DAMEN

THE *Marquette* FAMILY BOOK TWO

NATIONAL BESTSELLING AUTHOR

TRESSIE LOCKWOOD

AMIRA PRESS

DAMEN
The Marquette Family
Book Two

Amira Press
www.amirapress.com

CHAPTER ONE

Gideon's foot smashed through one of the boxes, and his ankle caught. He tried to yank it free but instead tumbled forward and fell flat on his face. Tasting blood on his tongue, he cursed and raised his head.

"I know I didn't just hear what I think I did, Gideon," his mother called from her room.

He grumbled under his breath. The walls were thinner here than the last place. Another curse, this one in his head. Then he felt guilty about disobeying his mother, so he turned it into "darn." That made him sound like a sissy. Maybe if he kept everything in his head, she wouldn't know. Then again, his mother had a way of reading his mind.

Another grunt, and he started digging through the boxes littering his room. Where was it? He knew he had packed the hoodie. His mother couldn't have found it and thrown it out like she threatened fifty million times.

No, please. Not that.

1

He ripped into the box marked "Gideon's Best Stuff—Don't Touch!!!!" The marker had run out on the last exclamation point. His mother had said it was because he was being too dramatic with the box labeling, and she wasn't going to buy more. He hadn't cared because he didn't have any more boxes to label.

Clothes everywhere, he finally found the hoodie, and ripped off the one she bought last week to replace with his favorite. So what, there were holes in both pockets, and the ends of the sleeves were ratty. He raised an arm to his nose and sniffed hard. Didn't stink either…not much.

Gideon tried zipping the jacket before he remembered a few teeth had fallen out of the zipper.

"Darn," he called loudly.

His mother laughed next door. "That's more like it."

He shook his head.

"Are you almost finished, Gideon? We can order some Chinese or whatever when we can see the light of day in all this stuff. I think I'm getting there. What about you?"

"Almost." He scanned his room. Well, three boxes were empty. Gideon shoved the messy pile of their contents aside and slid another box closer. He tore off the tape on the top and rummaged inside. The other most important thing he owned met his searching fingers, and he pulled it out. His mother didn't know he had found the article in her closet three years ago. She had probably forgotten, but this was the clue he had been looking for.

Gideon made space on the floor and smoothed the article out. The paper was worn around the edges, but he had been careful not to touch the middle parts too much. He knew the words by heart, but just in case, he traced them with his finger just above the paper.

There it was—*Marquette's*. That was the restaurant his dad owned with his two brothers, and it was here in their new city, New Orleans. Gideon took his time folding the article, but instead of slipping it back in the box, he folded it carefully and hid it inside his backpack.

A ringing started up in his mother's room, and Gideon tiptoed to the door. His mother was speaking to someone. Maybe he could sneak out now. He crept a little farther along the hall and froze to listen.

"Why are you calling?" she said. "I told you, it's over. I don't want to talk to you anymore."

Gideon frowned. That must his mother's ex-boyfriend. They had lived with him forever. His mom thought he didn't know, but Gideon knew. He used to hurt her, and Gideon promised himself when he was bigger, he'd stand up to that man and beat him up. His mother had finally left before that happened, and Gideon was glad.

"No," his mother was saying, and Gideon thought he heard tears in her voice. "I don't want that. I don't want—"

Even from where he stood in the hallway, Gideon picked up the shouting coming over the line. He gritted his teeth and raised the buds hanging around his neck to his ears. He hit the button on his cell phone, and music blocked out the world. Gideon hurried back to his room, pulled the backpack onto his shoulder, and crawled on hands and knees past his mother's bedroom door. Then he headed out.

Once Gideon was outside, he glanced up and down the street. Which way? Back in New York, all he had to do was go outside their apartment, and there were so many cars flying up and down the street. Getting a taxi was easy. Even if he found one here, would they pick up an eleven-year-old kid? He'd never tried on his own.

When he spotted cars passing at the end of the street, Gideon started that way. "Lucky," he whispered and pulled his ear buds out of his ears when he saw a taxi coming as soon as he reached the end. He waved for it, and breathed in relief when it actually stopped.

The driver rolled down the window and frowned doubtfully at Gideon. Then he glanced past him as if he expected Gideon's mother to appear. "Where are you going, kid?"

"Marquette's Restaurant," he said, trying to sound confident, but he heard a quiver in his voice on the end.

The man looked behind him again. "Where's your mom?"

"Never mind." Gideon tried to look taller and older. "I'm going. Will you take me, or not?"

An eyebrow rose, and the man made a rude noise. He pointed down the road with his chin. "Ten blocks that way. You don't need a taxi." The car peeled away from the curb.

"Ten blocks?" Gideon groaned. Well, if he wanted to see his dad, he guessed he better get moving, and who knew when his mother would find him missing and call his cell phone. Then he'd be in big trouble, and she might force him to come home. That couldn't happen. He had to see his dad just once at least.

Gideon started walking in the direction the taxi driver had pointed. Actually, he wanted to see his dad more than once. All Gideon's life, his mother had been telling him his dad was nice, that he was a good man. Gideon had tried to get her to say who he was, but she never would say. Then three years ago, he learned the truth. After that, he just knew if he could talk to his dad, they could be together, just the three of them, like a real family. Nobody would hurt his mother anymore because his dad would protect her.

"Maybe it'll happen today." He smiled thinking about it and walked faster. Yeah, today, his dad might move in with them, or they could move into his place. A warm feeling came over Gideon, and he pushed his earbuds in his ears, this time not to shut out the world but to dream. He couldn't wait.

The walk felt like it took forever, but at last Gideon stood across the street from the restaurant. He removed his ear buds and tucked them into his pocket. As he stared at the giant green letters that spelled out Marquette's Restaurant, his heart pounded so hard, he thought he would throw up. He tried to cross the street, but his feet wouldn't move. Cars rolled by, people laughed their way into the restaurant, and came out. Still he stood there, his eyes aching, his fingers clenching and unclenching at his sides.

He swallowed. Maybe this wasn't a good idea. Maybe he should go home. What if he was wrong and that picture of Damen Marquette that he'd caught his mom crying over didn't mean Damen was his dad at all. That hurt, and he felt moisture gathering in his eyes. He sucked in a breath and blew it out.

No! He is my dad. Damen Marquette is my dad, and I'm going to prove it to myself and everybody once and for all.

Finally, Gideon found the courage to cross the street and he walked up to the restaurant doors. With the sun still mostly up, he couldn't see through the glass without pressing his nose to it, so he took a chance and opened the door. Some people in fancy clothes walked ahead of him.

One man patted Gideon's fluffy curls. "Thanks, young man."

Gideon, feeling shy, just nodded, but he didn't intend

to hold the door for them. Well, it worked out in his favor anyway. He dropped low and followed the couple through the entrance, and when a woman in a black skirt and white shirt asked the people for their names, Gideon slipped by and hid behind a screen.

Crouching on one knee with his heart in his throat, Gideon glanced up at the screen. Old-fashioned scenes covered it, women in long dresses, men with tall hats, and horse-drawn carriages.

While he waited to calm down, he slowly became aware of the scent of food, and his empty stomach growled. Glasses clinked, and forks and knives scraped plates. People laughed all around him. He dropped to all fours and crept to the edge of the screen to peer around it. All over a huge room, there were tables with white tablecloths thrown over them, and it looked like every one of them was taken up with more people in fancy clothes.

Waiters and waitresses scurried about holding trays of food. From his level, Gideon couldn't see what kind of food it was, but he smelled it, and his mouth watered. He groaned. No, he had to focus. Where was his dad?

Shakily, he got to his feet and peered around. He stretched to his toes and craned his neck. There were a lot of men here, but most of them were in black. Why did they all have to wear the same colors? Wait a minute. His dad was an owner. He wouldn't serve the customers like some waiter, but where would he be? In the back, in an office or something?

Gideon's heart sank. If his dad was in an office somewhere, Gideon would have to either give up or ask for him. Coming here was hard enough, but he couldn't give up. He squared his shoulders and took a step forward.

"Where do you think you're going, ragamuffin?"

Gideon froze and looked up into the frowning face of a woman with blond hair and blue eyes. She might have been pretty if she didn't look so mean. Her hands on her hips, she blocked his view and his progress.

"I…" The words stuck in his throat. "I came…"

"I know what you came for," she snapped. Her gaze scraped over him from head to foot. "And you can go around back like all the rest."

The rest? He wondered who the rest were. There couldn't be more of his dad's kids. No, that was stupid. She couldn't *know* why he came. He wasn't the smartest kid, but he wasn't that stupid.

"I'm here to—"

"Around back!" She waved a hand to shoo him toward the door. Something told Gideon if he left now, he wouldn't find the courage to come again. He couldn't leave, not this close.

"Tiffany!" A man's voice cut across the grumpy one of the woman's, the man's voice deep but nicer. "We don't treat customers like that."

Gideon's heart raced as he waited for the man to come into view, and then the man stood beside the woman. He was tall and muscular, wearing the same clothes as the waiters, but he stood out with laughing green eyes and a nice smile. He looked a lot like the picture of the man in Gideon's pocket.

"But Stefan, look at him," the woman complained. "He's a scruffy—"

"Enough, Tiff. Go back to your duties, please." The voice was still gentle but firm. Tiff glowered at Gideon once more, and then spun on her heel to stomp away. Gideon blew out a breath. He looked at the man again. So big, surely he couldn't be as nice as Gideon thought.

"Hey, buddy, you here alone?"

Gideon blinked. "Me?"

"Yes, you."

Gideon frowned. He remembered how the taxi driver treated him, looking past him, waiting for his mother to appear. "I've got money. I'm not a raga-something. Whatever she said." He dug into his pocket and dragged out his allowance, what he had intended to use for the ride over there.

The man nodded. "Very good, Mr…?"

Gideon drew himself up. "Gideon Burk."

"Mr. Burk, I'm Stefan Marquette, and I'll be happy to show you to your table."

Gideon's mouth fell open. His eyes widened, and he didn't move from the spot. He stared, taking in the man in more detail. This was his uncle, his real live uncle! He had never had an uncle before. There was only his mom and his grandfather, and that old man didn't like him very much. The feeling was mutual. *Uncle Stefan.* He tested the words in his head a few times. He liked it.

"Mr. Burk, are you ready?"

"Y-yes, sir."

Uncle Stefan led him to a table, and Gideon dropped into a chair and then dumped his backpack on the one next to it. His uncle gave him a menu. He opened it up, and his eyes bugged. No way could he afford anything. His heart sank, but his uncle hadn't left the table. He waited for Gideon to order something.

"I…I guess I'll have the chocolate layer cake and a cola," he mumbled. His stomach rumbled again, but with the music playing and people talking all around, his uncle wouldn't hear. Gideon had a huge appetite, even if he was still pretty skinny.

"Are you allergic to anything?" Uncle Stefan asked.

"Huh?"

"Allergies?"

Gideon didn't really know what allergies had to do with anything, but he didn't have any, so he just shook his head. Uncle Stefan took the menu and disappeared. Gideon sighed and looked around. He still hadn't spotted his dad yet, which worried him. Too much time had passed. He pulled his cell phone from his pocket and checked the screen. No texts yet.

After a short while, Uncle Stefan showed up again with a tray. He set a plate on the table in front of Gideon. "Cheeseburger with the works, French fries, and a cola."

Gideon started in fear. "I didn't order this."

"Eat up," Uncle Stefan insisted. "It's on the house. I'll bring your cake a little later."

"On the house?"

"Free," his uncle emphasized.

"Are you sure?"

Uncle Stefan smiled and winked. "Positive. Go on. Give it a try. Our chefs are the best in New Orleans."

Gideon couldn't help it. He stuffed the burger into his mouth and took a huge bite. Flavors he couldn't figure out danced on his tongue, but it didn't matter. All he knew was it was better than fast food and any of the restaurants his mother had taken him to in the past. He bit and chewed as fast as he could. Between bites, he stuffed French fries into his mouth and sipped his soda.

"I'm guessing it's good," Uncle Stefan teased.

"Yeah, thanks a lot."

Then Gideon forgot the food entirely. One of the double doors with circle windows in it opened, and his dad appeared. Gideon followed him with his gaze as he stopped at various tables, talking with the customers, laughing with them. He shook the hands of the men and said something that made the women's faces turn red, but they all looked happier after talking to his dad.

Out of the corner of his eye, Gideon saw his uncle leave the table. Uncle Stefan signaled to his dad, and the two stood together with their backs turned away from Gideon. Then the both of them looked around at him. Gideon slipped to the side, teetering on the edge of his seat. Why were they looking at him? Had they found him out? Had his mother called? No, that was impossible. She didn't know where he was.

Both men started toward him. He jumped to his feet, a little dizzy. The thought to run washed over him, but just like outside when he first got there, he couldn't move. What if… What if…

His dad stood before him, towering over him and smiling. He laid a heavy but gentle hand on top of Gideon's curls. "Hey, there, bud."

Bud? No one had ever called him bud. The word was weird, but it was okay, he guessed. Since it was his dad.

"Why don't you have a seat and finish your food?"

Gideon swallowed and sank into his chair. To his surprise, his dad sat down too. Gideon ducked his head and fiddled with a fry, but then he peeked up at his dad. He looked exactly like his picture, maybe a little older. His hair was neater than in the picture, dark, and his glasses were smaller. He couldn't believe his dad wore glasses. Maybe he should believe it. Gideon was supposed to, but he kept breaking or losing them. His vision wasn't so bad now, but his mother said if he wasn't careful, it would get worse. Gideon had always felt he looked like a nerd, but his dad didn't look bad at all. Those women seemed to like him.

"What's your name?" his dad asked. "I'm Damen."

"D-Damen," he said softly. His mother would kill him if he called her by her name. "My name's Gideon."

"Wow, cool name. I like it."

"T-thanks." Gideon ducked his head again, and to his disgust and shame tears fell down his cheeks. He scrubbed an arm across his eyes. What a wuss. Why the heck was he crying at a time like this? His dad would think he was an idiot.

"It's okay."

The deep voice settled him down somehow, and Gideon sniffed.

His dad squeezed his shoulder. "If you're in trouble, we can help find you somewhere warm and dry."

Gideon laughed. He had been mad when the woman near the door insulted him, but he didn't blame his dad for thinking he was a bum. The jacket was pretty bad. "I'm not homeless. I've got a mom, and she's nice most of the time, except when I do something stupid. Then she lectures me until I think my ears will bleed."

His dad chuckled and crossed his eyes. "Moms are like that."

A burst of joy rose in Gideon. He leaned forward. "What about dads? Do they lecture?"

His dad bent closer to him and looked around as if he was about to share something top secret. He put a hand next to his mouth to keep others from hearing. "Dads help start the stuff that make the moms lecture."

Gideon's eyes bugged. "You, too?"

"Me? Of course."

"I knew it!" Gideon's voice came out kind of hoarse, but he didn't worry about it. He felt bolder, as if he could tell his dad the truth now that he'd met him. The two of them could get into all sorts of stuff just for fun, but most of all, his dad looked muscular enough to protect his mom. Maybe he was even as nice as his eyes looked so he would never hit her. That was the most important. Okay, he'd made his decision. He'd tell him right now. Gideon breathed deep a few times.

"I'm the best dad ever. Just ask my daughter. Right, Nita?"

Gideon hadn't noticed the little girl walking over. She stood next to his dad, and his dad touched her back with one hand as she leaned dramatically over the table. Long, dark hair splayed on the table, and she groaned.

"Daddy, I'm hungry."

Gideon blinked. Daddy? The article never mentioned he had a daughter. She looked younger than Gideon and neither black nor white. His dad was white, and his mom black, so he looked like a mix of the two, but this girl didn't. Maybe she wasn't his real daughter.

The girl raised her head and studied him. Gideon tried not to notice she had the same nose as him and his dad and the same lips. "Who's this dirty boy, Daddy?"

"Who's dirty?" Gideon snapped, balling his fists at his sides.

"Easy, you two," his dad said. "Nita, don't be rude. Gideon, I'm sorry. She gets a little cranky when she's hungry. Nita, I'll get Shada to make you something."

"No," the girl whined, "I want pizza."

"I'm on duty, sweetheart, and I told you we would get pizza tomorrow night."

"Pizza, now, Daddy! Why can't we have pizza now?"

Gideon blinked over and over at her. He kept waiting for his dad to tell her to stop being a big baby. If he'd acted like that, all his mother would have to do was look at him with one eyebrow raised, and he'd pull himself together. No way would he test her the way this girl was doing.

Gideon didn't like the girl, but as he watched, his dad bent over and kissed the top of Nita's head while he rubbed her back. "Okay, you win. I'll get one of the waiters to run out and get a pizza. You can eat it in the office so the customers don't think we serve it here."

"Yay!" Nita bounced up and down, grinning.

His dad drew her into his arms and hugged her tight. Gideon didn't know why, but he felt like the world was crumbling around him. All of sudden, it seemed as if everyone laughing in the restaurant were laughing at him. A glass wall slammed down between him and his dad, keeping him on one side and his dad with Nita on the other. Gideon's chest hurt.

His dad was saying something, but it was hard to hear. Gideon thought it might be "enjoy your meal" or whatever. His dad stood up, but he didn't touch Gideon again. He just smiled, took Nita's hand, and led her away from the table. Gideon watched them get farther and farther away. The restaurant grew bigger with each step. He dug into his pocket and threw all the money he had on the table and walked out of the restaurant.

Gideon pushed the ear buds into his ears and blasted his music. Before he put his phone away, he checked the texts. Just as he thought, his mom wanted to know where he was. He sniffed a few times and texted back.

"I'm fine."

Another message came in, but he didn't look at it. He dropped the phone into his pocket and started a slow pace toward home. The music flowed over him, and he let it sink in from his head to his body, and especially to that place deep down inside that was tight right now.

I won't cry. I already did that. I'm not a sissy.

At least he had gotten to see his dad once. That would have to be enough. So they wouldn't be a family. Big deal. His dad already had a kid, a little daughter, who even though Gideon hated her, was pretty. His dad had everything he needed, brothers, a kid, a business, and money. He didn't need Gideon too or his mom.

A sob escaped Gideon, but he suppressed it. He tried to zip the jacket, but the two sides came apart from the bottom as soon as he reached the top. Maybe he should throw this thing away. He clutched it in his fists and ducked his head until his chin touched his chest. All he could do was watch his feet and keep walking.

His dad had talked to him. He had smiled and touched the top of Gideon's head. *That's enough.*

CHAPTER TWO

Heaven fired off another text and frowned when her son didn't answer. Where the hell was he? Gideon knew better than to ignore her texts or her calls. She studied the screen of her phone a few minutes, waiting. Nothing. Of course, he could have his music blasting in his ears. He was famous for that, but she had gotten onto him about checking every so often.

Pissed, she bypassed the last box she needed to unpack and marched next door to his room. The disaster area that met her gaze wasn't a surprise, but it did set her off even more. That scrawny butt boy had lied to her, saying he was almost done. Well, he could forget about Chinese food. Whatever they had at that tiny storefront down the street was what he was getting, and it wasn't going to be fancy if she had to cook it.

She slipped into her shoes and stepped out of the apartment. Right away, the humidity of the South hit her,

15

making it hard to breathe. The New Orleans weather would take some getting used to, but at least the winters would be milder. New York snow was no joke.

Heaven manipulated the screens on her phone until she came to the tracking app she had installed not too long ago. Gideon hated her having the ability to find him wherever he went, but too bad. He was eleven, and they were in a new city. That boy's head was in the clouds a lot, and she wasn't risking him being safe. Period. He could get over it. Besides, she didn't follow him around, spying on him. The app was for times like now, when he didn't answer her. Gideon could be stubborn just like his dad.

She had started walking down the street, but at the thought of Damen, she came to a stop. Her heart hammered for no reason. *Get a grip, Heaven.* This was why she had come to New Orleans in the first place, to finally tell Damen about his son. Over the years, she had been tracking him and knew about his marriage and the ending of it. Heaven knew about the little girl, Anita, and the restaurant. She wasn't worried about Damen being able to love her baby as much as he loved his daughter. What concerned her was *would* he. Would Damen accept Gideon?

Heaven got moving again, following the little arrow that told her the direction of Gideon's phone. She heaved a sigh. Right now, worried about Gideon and what he was doing, and Damen and whether he would accept Gideon, she couldn't focus on the beauty of New Orleans. On some level, she was aware of how narrow Saint Louis Street was and how it seemed like every building had balconies with wrought iron railings and hanging plants to decorate them. There was a lot of history here and uniqueness of the South, but she had plenty of time to explore once she found her son and gave him a piece of her mind.

The closer Heaven drew to the arrow, she began to realize Gideon was moving in her direction, slower, but still making progress. She glanced up at the sky and caught sight of the sun dipping low on the horizon. A ball of orange, much less painful from its position but still beautiful, she realized it would be dark soon. Worry stirred in her. Gideon must be hungry. He ate like a horse but didn't gain an ounce of weight. She was thin as well, but that had more to do with the relationship she had come out of. Gaining weight wasn't an option.

She cringed, thinking of her ex-boyfriend. Now that she had made the move to New Orleans, she wondered how she had stood the abuse for so long. Maybe it was because Leon had never done it in front of Gideon. Her son didn't know how bad it had gotten, and she had hidden the bruises from him and her dad, during the infrequent times she saw him.

At first, she'd wanted Gideon and her dad to have a relationship, but when it became clear it would never be normal just like her own relationship with her dad, she gave up. Always hoping something would give, she kept visiting the man, but he was cold and as distant as ever. That's why she hoped with everything inside her that Gideon and Damen could meet and get along. Damen was different. Yeah, he was smart—a certified genius actually—but he had always been nice and kind of introverted. Damn, she had loved that man, and she couldn't have asked anything more of the time they had spent together than to walk away with his baby. Gideon would be a reminder of him forever.

When the two arrows were about on top of each other, Heaven looked up and scanned the street. Gideon walked with his head down on the opposite side of the road. Heaven stepped around a parked car and checked for oncoming traffic before crossing over. She stood in Gideon's path and let her son bump into her.

He staggered back and started around her. "Sorry."

"Gideon!" She snatched a bud from his ear.

He jumped and raised his head. Heaven's heart constricted when she saw the look in his big brown eyes, her eyes. Then he wrinkled his nose and the sadness disappeared. He hunched his shoulders the way he always did when he was guilty of something.

"Where have you been, boy?" she demanded, putting her hands on her hips.

"Sorry, Mom. I was just walking around, looking at stuff. I got lost a little."

"Lost!" She laid a hand on his shoulder and glanced in the direction he'd come from. Suddenly, she realized where they were, so close to Marquette's she thought she could smell the food. No way would her son have gone there, would he? Of course not. He didn't know who his dad was because she had never told him, and she was hiding the reason for their move until she met with Damen herself. This must be a coincidence. She sighed in relief, having eased her mind. "I told you not to go off without telling me where you're going, Gideon. This isn't New York. We had friends and neighbors who know us and who could look out for you. We don't know anyone here."

He opened his mouth, but then snapped it closed and lowered her gaze. "Yes, ma'am."

"That's what I thought." She noticed his jacket and frowned. "Ugh, Gideon, how many times do I have to tell you to stop wearing that thing? If you're going to hang on to it at least stop wearing it in the street. It makes me look like

I don't take care of you, and you have a brand new hoodie."

"I know." He seemed to consider what she said, which was a first, and it looked like he was remembering something. "You're right."

"I know I'm right." She grinned. "I'm not going to force you to throw it away. Just have mercy on your mother for a change."

"Okay." His fingers fiddled with the ear buds, and she rolled her eyes. "Can I listen to my music now?"

"Fine. Go ahead." They walked alongside each other with Heaven wrapping her arm around his narrow shoulders.

She stroked her son's curls once before he could brush her hand away. The texture of it was softer and silkier than her own, although hers wasn't bad with a little help from a flat iron. Gideon got his hair from a mixture of hers and Damen's, but she suspected Damen's hair grew a lot faster. That had to be the case as Gideon's hair grew like a damn weed. He hated barbershops, so she didn't take him as often as she would like to. Not that she minded much. She loved his hair and everything about her son's appearance.

Gideon's smooth skin was lighter than her chocolate brown but darker than his dad's, even when Damen's was tanned. To her eyes—a mother's eyes—he was the cutest kid in the world, and she loved him with all her heart. Heaven would make any sacrifice for him, but she longed more than anything for him to get to know Damen.

Because she had loved Damen almost twelve years ago during their brief affair, she had never let either of the two men she had been with since get too close to her son. Maybe she had been wrong, but the last one, Leon, wasn't worth Gideon's affection either way. Everything would change with Damen.

Heaven wrung her hands. They were moist, and she wiped them on her skirt but didn't feel it did any good. Not when her underarms felt damp, putting her deodorant to the test, and her blouse stuck to her back. None of it had anything to do with the warm weather. In fact, with a cool breeze blowing off the Mississippi River, she should feel fine. She didn't. Nerves threatened to send her screaming down the street like a maniac.

Not even that serious, Heaven. She told herself that, but it did nothing to calm her down. The fact was, this was serious. She'd made the decision and was here outside Damen's restaurant.

Thoughts like *what if he isn't the same man* swirled through her head. Logic said of course he wasn't the same. Everyone matured over the years, and Damen's circumstances had altered drastically. Who hadn't heard of money changing people? When she knew Damen, he'd been working his way through college. She learned later, that was just before his breakthrough when he started a stockphoto website with his brothers. Over the next decade, the company Damen and his brothers owned had made them billionaires. Talk about terrified of stepping out of the woodwork. She should have done it before he became rich.

Heaven noticed the sign again she had spotted the day before when her courage had failed her. Yesterday, she had come to the restaurant with the determination to march in and demand to see Damen. Then she'd seen the sign, saw the elegance, the important-looking clientele, and whatever backbone she had grown, burst into powder and blew away on the breeze. She had fled, but she had recalled seeing the

Help Wanted sign for wait staff.

Could she? Should she? No, that was stupid. If she applied for a job as a waitress, Damen would recognize her right off the bat. Then she would look shady. Well, either way, she needed to get her butt inside and see what was what.

Heaven grabbed the door handle and opened the door. A breeze stirred her hair, and the scent of some type of meat wafted out, along with the scent of something sweet. She had expected to find a bunch of customers laughing and eating at the tables and waitresses whizzing about, but the place appeared empty. No music played, but she picked up the clink of dishes from somewhere behind the door with the porthole windows.

Heaven braved a few more steps into the restaurant and noted the sea of tables had their chairs upended on top of them, but at the far side of the room, a woman was taking them down and covering the tables with white tablecloths. Heaven might have come at a good time after all, when they weren't so busy. Damen might have a minute to talk.

Voices reached her, and then the porthole windowed door opened. A man strode through, followed by several women. "This way. If you'll all take a seat, we can get down to the interview."

Heaven stilled. She recognized the man, although she had never met him in person. This was Creed, the oldest brother. Eyes that were identical to Damen's but cold as ice focused on her. Whatever courage she'd dredged up earlier disappeared that quickly.

"You're here for the interview?" he asked. "Join the others at the tables. I've already given a quick tour, the last place being the kitchen. If you were on time..."

Heaven floundered between telling him the truth and

getting the heck out of there. His ugly attitude riled her temper, but she had learned over the years not to argue too much. Mouthing off got her hit. Not that she thought this man would do that to her, but he might be the abusive type. She had no idea.

"Hello?" he grumped.

A black woman in a chef's uniform came from another direction and sashayed in front of Creed. She whacked him in the chest. "Jeez, you're grumpy today. How do you think you're going to get any of these applicants to want to work here? Get a grip."

Several gasps rose from the scattered group, along with Heaven's. The woman kept moving toward what Heaven realized now was the kitchen. Creed's gaze followed her every step of the way, and Heaven drew in a sharp breath. She had never in her life seen a man look like that. For a few amazing moments, Creed had stared at the woman like she was his entire world, and even though the look wasn't directed at Heaven, it stole her breath. He loved this woman, whoever she was. Heaven would give anything to have a man look at her like Creed had stared at the chef.

Maybe Heaven should wait a little bit longer to reveal herself. *It's just curiosity, not me hoping he'll be like...* She shut her thoughts down and rushed to grab a seat amid the other women. While Creed shuffled through some papers he held in a blue folder, he wasn't watching all of them. Heaven peered around to find every one of the women there to be interviewed checking their hair and makeup.

Are they serious? She shook her head. This was a job, not a bride selection ceremony. She kicked herself mentally for being a hypocrite. The Marquettes were gorgeous, single men, and even if Heaven hadn't been in the market for a man, she noticed too. In fact, she knew something inside her strained for the moment when Damen showed himself.

She didn't think she still loved him or anything. Those feelings had died down years ago, but he would probably always hold a special place in her heart because he was Gideon's father.

Creed looked up from his papers and cleared his throat. The murmur that had risen with his distraction quieted down. "Uh, I apologize for my earlier gruffness," he said, surprising Heaven with his honesty. "My fiancée keeps me in line, as you can see."

Several grumbles of disappointment rose in various directions. Heaven kept quiet.

"If you are hired here at Marquette's," Creed continued, "you should know we're fair and generous. That is my and my brothers' policy. However, if you're the sensitive type, it might not be a good fit."

He had the nerve to look sheepish, and the kitchen door opened to emit another man. He slapped Creed on the back. "Yes, because Shada isn't around him twenty-four seven, you'll have to learn he's all bark and no bite. Don't worry, though. I'll look out for you all. I'm Damen Marquette, by the way."

Heaven hadn't needed to be introduced. She recognized him from the second he stepped through the door. Same brilliant green eyes, same sexy smile. His raven black hair was styled flashier than he used to wear it, but the order was still there. The way he had of pushing his glasses up his nose with two fingers, why on earth did she think that was so hot? The move got her every time and drew her in like a fishing reel. She had never told him about her weakness, but back then, Damen would never have used it against her anyway.

Today, Heaven saw something different in Damen. He flirted, with every single woman, meeting their gazes, firing that heart-stopping smile at them. Was it an act? Surely, it had to be. Her Damen would never have— She stopped the thought cold. *Not even worth correcting, just let it go.*

Damen walked around the room shaking hands and introducing himself to each woman—and the two men, probably just to save face. When he reached Heaven, she stiffened, waiting for him to recognize her. He held out his hand, and she hesitated, quivering a little. She met his gaze and touched his hand. With his much bigger one, he made her feel small.

She braced for recognition, but when it didn't come, she said, "Heaven."

His eyebrows rose, and he smiled. "I feel like I've heard that before."

Creed dragged him away from her when he held her hand too long. "Yeah, it's the place I'm sending you early if you don't quit wasting my time. Now, ladies and gentlemen…"

The interview swirled around her. She gave mechanical answers to questions asked. Heaven had sat in on countless practice sessions when she worked at the university for one of the professors at NYU. By now, she didn't have to think, which was good because all she could do was replay the instance of her meeting Damen again after more than a decade. He didn't remember her, the woman he'd slept with. Sure, neither of them had been a virgin at the time, but her experience wasn't all that, and he'd said neither was his. Shouldn't he have recalled the damn black woman he slept with?

No. Damen had always dated outside his race. Her brown skin wasn't a big deal to him, but it hurt like hell that she was just another face. He'd changed all right. The nerdy man, who kept his nose stuck in a book most of the time was gone. That didn't mean he wouldn't be a good dad to Gideon, but she still wasn't sure.

"Heaven."

She started at Creed's voice and looked over at him.

"Do you mind joining me in my office?"

She hesitated and then followed him through the kitchen, down a short hall, and through another door. This was the time to come clean if she was going to do it. Creed could call his brother in, and she could talk to him and tell him the truth.

"Have a seat." Creed gestured to a chair, and she sank into it. Her throat dry, she kept swallowing. He moved to a counter across the room and poured water into a glass and then handed it to her

"Thanks," she said softly and took a sip. Drinking gave her an excuse not to look up at him, and she welcomed it. This man intimidated the hell out of her. How could she introduce the subject of being his brother's baby mama? Thinking of it almost brought a groan to her lips, but maybe Creed already suspected something, calling her back here when he hadn't singled out any of the others.

"Who are you really?" Creed said.

Heaven choked. Creed moved at lightening speed to pound her back too hard, and she waved him away, her eyes burning. She took a moment before speaking to keep from stuttering, but before she could gather her words, Creed headed her off.

"I apologize. That sounded like an accusation. What I meant to say, your answers, your manner, everything about you says professional. You're not a waitress by trade, are you?"

She couldn't respond.

"Let me be clear," he said. "I will never turn away a person for the bogus reason of they're 'overqualified.' If you need the job, you need the job. Period. Whether I think you can do a good job is what's important to me. You might have been CEO to a Fortune 500 company last week and got laid off."

She grinned. "I get your point, but I'm so not an ex-bigwig."

Creed leaned back in his chair. "Good to know."

"I'm…" She hesitated. *Truth, lie, truth, lie… Delayed truth, not really a lie.* "I've worked in the area of library science and English literature." There, that wasn't a lie. The thing was, she *still* worked in her chosen field, and the hours were convenient maybe to working for a short while as a waitress. How hard could it be?

He nodded. "Understood. I'm willing to hire you on a trial basis. Staying depends on how fast you learn and how well you adapt. One thing I need to make abundantly clear."

This was her last chance to come clean. "Yes?"

"My brother. He's never serious about anyone. I don't want you to think if he gives you special attention it means anything."

She bristled, not meaning to let the offense show. "Because I'm beneath him?"

Creed grinned.

"Uh, sorry. I didn't mean—"

"It's fine. I don't mind my employees speaking their mind either, even if it's to me or one of my brothers. No, what I mean is Damen's not in the market for a serious relationship. That's just the way it is right now, and I don't want anyone hurt. You don't have to worry. He will not cross the line."

Heaven heard the crack of Creed's knuckles as he

clenched a hand into a fist atop the desk. Her own nails dug into her palms.

"If you ever feel he has, tell me, and I'll crack his head for him."

"Um, that won't be necessary. I think I can handle myself."

He nodded. "Okay, then. Fill out the application I gave you out front, and if your references check out—even if they have nothing to do with the restaurant business—I'll give you a call."

"Thank you."

Heaven slipped out of the office and back into the hall leading to the kitchen. One part of her wanted to go find Damen. The other wanted to hit the street running. Instead, some sense of hope led her to the dining room and to a chair away from everyone. She sat down and filled out the application with names and numbers of friends she knew would not only give her great references but keep her business hers, like the fact that she had moved to New Orleans with a job in hand.

When the time was right, she and Damen would have their discussion. Nothing would change the past. Her dad had told her she needed to let Damen pursue his dreams and not be tied down with her son. Of all people, her dad, an English professor at NYU, had become Damen's mentor back then. Since she and her dad kept their distances from each other most of the time, she didn't think Damen ever knew. The day she came home and told her dad about the baby, she had it solidified as to how much more her dad thought of Damen than he thought of her.

"Either get rid of the baby, or raise it yourself, Heaven," he'd said. "That boy's been through enough in his life, and he doesn't need all his dreams wiped out by your mistake."

As if she had gotten herself pregnant, or she had forced Damen not to use a condom, her dad's words went straight through her. Still, since she loved Damen, she had agreed— for *him*. She would show her baby enough love for both of them and raise him differently than her dad had done with her. She would hug and kiss him like her dad didn't do with her.

So far, Heaven had kept her promise to herself and to Gideon, but now Damen was successful. Nothing she did could hurt him, and she had figured maybe, just maybe, if he was still a decent man, he could be a good dad to Gideon. Heaven might not have known a great example of a dad, but Gideon might. Her background made her cautious, but damn it, she hoped with every fiber of her being.

Heaven reached the street after turning in her application and walked toward home. The next step was to wait for Creed's call. Then another chapter of her life would begin.

CHAPTER THREE

"So it was you, huh?"

Heaven turned around to find the little blond leaning against the doorframe. "Excuse me?"

The woman, Tiff, if Heaven remembered correctly, flipped a long ponytail off her shoulder. She started toward Heaven. "Creed hired you and those other two girls."

Heaven shrugged. "And one of the men, I hear. So what?"

She didn't need to ask so what. Heaven already saw it coming a mile off. She knew the attitude. Tiff thought since she had been at Marquette's longer and had seniority, she could dictate a few things. Heaven was supposed to listen and fall in line.

"I told the other two already," Tiff said. "Damen's mine. Hands off. If you try anything to get his attention on you, I'm getting you fired."

"Wow, and here I thought you were going to say you

get first dibs on hours." Heaven had already talked to Creed about needing time for classes. The classes were Gideon's, his tutoring sessions before school started for the year, and of course she worked for one of the local colleges. The job was a step down in her father's opinion, but Heaven would have taken any position to get to New Orleans. "And correct me if I'm wrong, but I believe Creed told me Damen is never serious with anyone. Maybe you should have a talk with Damen about where you stand."

Tiff's faced reddened, and Heaven raised her eyebrows waiting for a comeback. The woman floundered for a few moments longer, and then she stomped a foot. "Just watch your step, and I mean it."

"I'm sure you do, girlfriend, but I don't like threats. I've had my fill of them for several lifetimes. You"—Heaven flicked a finger up and down in the air to encompass Tiff's length—"couldn't scare me if you tried."

This time, Tiff made a choked sound. Heaven slammed her locker door and moved past Tiff. She knew she'd made an enemy, but she didn't care. Just like she said, Leon had threatened her many times, and he followed up with painful action. No tiny little gold-digger would make her lose sleep for an instant. Besides, she wasn't looking to get involved with Damen again. That led to hurt she didn't need.

Creed had chosen the lunchtime stretch to be when Heaven could be trained for the waitressing job. She still held out hope this would be a piece of cake—take people's orders, relay them to the kitchen staff, and collect payment. Maybe there would even be tips.

"Heaven, you're shadowing Karey today," Creed told her.
"Got it."

"Okay, this job can be fun with the guys," Karey said with

a smile, "or it can be a pain in the ass. The real exciting stuff happens at night, though, so if you get a shift then, you're lucky."

"How do you mean?"

Karey closed her eyes as if she tasted something good. There was a delicious scent of Crawfish *Étouffée* in the air, a spicy stew of crawfish, vegetables, and a dark roux, served over rice. Heaven didn't think that had anything to do with it. "Stefan sings. Not every night, just once in a while, but there's also Creed acting like an angry bear when his girlfriend is called for compliments to the chef and gets hit on instead. Then there's…"

She kept ticking off the points, and Heaven found herself wishing she could work the night shift, but she had to think about Gideon. He had mentioned something about a class on self-defense and one for basketball at the community center. Those were at night, but she would have to look into it.

"Well, let's get started." Karey pushed through to the dining room, and the jazz Heaven had been hearing grew a tad louder. The hum of voices stirred the air, and she was surprised to see every table filled with patrons.

"Wow, it's busy in here even during the middle of the day."

"It's the guys."

"You mean the Marquette brothers?"

"Yeah, they're all sexy and rich. Most people haven't come close to a billionaire before, so they like to experience it at least once. Then there's the food…" Karey pointed. "From that table all the way over to the one with the lady in polka dots is our section."

Nerves started in Heaven's belly. "Which ones?"

Karey whipped out a floor map. "Handy, right? Here,

take a look."

Heaven breathed a sigh of relief. The map had a clear layout of the entire floor on the front and even the smaller rooms on the second floor on the back of it. All the tables were marked with numbers and sections, so the waitress would know which she was responsible for.

"You'll need to memorize this, but we keep it so we can double check. There's no rush to be perfect at Marquette's. You just have to do your best and follow the rules Creed has set down."

"I've got you so far."

Heaven followed Karey and watched as the woman served for the first half hour. The fact that she had taken no more than a handful of orders from patrons who were eating light with choices like Louisiana shrimp served cold over a bed of fresh romaine and special house blend dressing or a corned beef and sauerkraut with thousand island dressing and melted swiss cheese boosted Heaven's confidence even more.

I've got this.

Then everything changed. Someone snapped or maybe they clapped, and Heaven swiveled around to see what it was. Creed stood just inside the dining room. A waiter glided to him, and Creed spoke a few quiet words. The waiter nodded and headed to where Heaven stood with Karey. She tensed, but the man was looking at Karey.

"Emergency call for you," he said. "Your mom."

"Heaven."

She started and glanced up into green eyes full of mischief.

"Looks like it's you and me," Damen said in a tone that didn't need to sound so damn sexy, as he strode up to her.

"You…and me? Why?"

"Because Karey is going home, and she won't be back." He leaned closer to her, crowding her space for an instant. "Looks like I'll be your new teacher."

Heaven wrinkled her nose and spun away. "I think I know everything I need to."

"Really?" Her statement seemed to intrigue the bastard. She expected him to add on a sexual innuendo, but he just smiled. The man didn't need to talk dirty or to hint at it when his presence exuded mind-numbing sexuality by itself.

Damen watched her as she handled the orders. Having his gaze constantly on her wracked her nerves, and each time she raised a glass to refresh it with water, the stupid thing rocked a little. When Heaven bumped a glass of wine over, staining the white tablecloth, Damen tugged her away and signaled for other staff to take her place. He found a quieter corner and squeezed her hand, but she yanked it away.

"Hey, calm down," he said softly.

Being this close, she picked up a hint of aftershave and spotted a light dusting of hair along his jawline. Damen had always been clean-shaven, but he had said he remained so by shaving every day. Her fingers itched to touch the stubble, but she curled them into her palms. What the heck was she thinking? She wasn't attracted to him anymore.

"I'm sorry," she mumbled. "I should get back there and clean up."

"Don't worry about it. Tiff's got it," he assured her. "But you look like you're wound tight. I want you to do a mental exercise."

She blinked up at him. "A what?"

"A mental exercise. Come on, now close your eyes."

She backed up a step. "Um, no."

Two fingers pushed his glasses higher. She groaned inwardly.

"Heaven, do you think I'm in the habit of molesting my employees?"

"Who said anything about you doing something to me?"

"So you're *not* scared of me?" He smirked, waiting for her answer.

Heaven studied his handsome face and recalled times they had laughed together in the library, hushed by the librarian and threatened of being thrown out. Damen had grabbed her hand and pulled her to the political science section of all places. At the end of the row, with people on both sides just feet away, he would kiss her. Then his face would be so red with embarrassment. They were older now, and Damen was probably way more experienced, but no, she wasn't scared of him.

"I'm not," she said.

He nodded. "So close your eyes."

She did. Her pulse raced, and her hands shook while she clutched them, but it had zero to do with the restaurant and all to do with the man in front of her. He didn't touch her, thank goodness, but his low voice guided her through the brief exercise. To Heaven's surprise, she found herself calming down.

"Now, I want you to say, none of my tasks are important."

"But—"

"Say it," he encouraged gently.

She did.

"My survival is independent to this job."

She repeated his words. He was such a nerd, and her heart warmed.

"Okay, open your eyes. Good?"

34

Heaven looked around. They had only stood behind the screen for at most a minute, but she did feel better. "I can't believe that worked. Are you a voodoo doctor now?"

He chuckled. "Yes, how did you know?"

"It's in the eyes," she teased.

They laughed together.

"You're different, Damen."

His eyebrows rose. "Really?"

Crap, she'd screwed up. "I mean I…"

"Read up on us like everyone else, I assume. Well, don't believe everything you read in the tabloids. I'm a nice guy. I haven't seduced a hundred virgins."

"Oh, is that what they say?"

"A hundred, two…"

She shook her head and returned to work. Thank all that was good and holy Damen backed off enough for her to get accustomed to the routine. She was starting to think she could do this with the best of them even when her feet started hurting. Heaven had withstood greater pain that was for sure.

"Heaven," Tiff called excitedly, "party of eight in your area. Get on it."

Heaven frowned. "I don't remember you being made my boss." She glanced over to her area and found Tiff was right. Four of the patrons were big strapping men with guts, probably not the type to eat light. She swallowed and headed over with a smile. "Good afternoon, ladies and gentlemen. Can I start you off with something to drink?"

"No, we always get the usual," the man at the head of the table said.

Heaven poised her pen above her pad. Just what the heck was the usual? Turned out he had only been drawing in a breath. The man fired off an order of food that made her head spin, heavy dishes, meat-centered dishes, extra sides. If this was the usual, how were their hearts still ticking? Gravy, sauce, beef, starches, no vegetables, thanks, and start them off with beer.

She cringed. "Let me run that back to you to make sure I got it right."

The man waved his hand. "No, don't bother. If you miss anything, I'll just send you back while we start on what we get."

"Uh, fine."

Heaven turned in the order, and when she got the call that her order was up, she pushed through to the kitchen to grab it. When she walked in, a wave of heat hit her in the face, bringing about beads of moisture on her forehead. Kitchen staff zipped all over the place, ducking and dodging each other. Heaven ignored them and looked toward the counter. She staggered a little. That huge platter couldn't be hers, could it?

Someone bumped her from behind, and she glanced around to find Tiff's glaring face. "What are you waiting for, Heaven. I had those guys last week. They'll kick up a dust if you don't get a move on."

Heaven knew this bitch would love that, but she figured Tiff was right. She strode over to the tray and tried to lift it. Her arm muscles quivered. She tried sliding it to the edge and raising it that way. The whole thing tilted, but the rubber inside kept the plates from sliding.

I can't do it. Panic started in her chest. She could feel Tiff's eyes on her, waiting for her to fail. Trying harder wouldn't work. Upper body strength had never been her forte, and damn it, she'd never needed it with her type of work.

The tray tilted some more, but she wouldn't give up. If it all tumbled to the floor, there would be a lot of food to prepare all over again.

"What are you doing?"

She started, and a strong arm came around her. Damen righted the tray with one big hand. She peered up at him. "I'm so sorry. I can't hold it. I'm not strong enough."

"Of course not. We have servers for that."

Her mouth fell open. "Huh?"

"Servers who are strong enough to wield these trays. I wouldn't expect you to do it. All you need to do is to grab one of them, and he would carry the food to the table for you. Come on. I'll take it and help you."

They moved past Tiff, who stepped aside. Heaven deliberately touched Damen's arm while looking at Tiff. "Thank you so much, Damen. You're so strong."

Tiff appeared to have burst a few capillaries. Heaven was pretty sure she read "you bitch" in the waitress's mouthed comment. She supposed soon she would be called into the boss's office and fired on the spot. Heaven almost laughed at the thought. Tiff was one of those people who were all talk.

The rest of the work day went along fine, and Heaven found herself having finished the day without killing herself or anybody else. She said good night to everybody and hurried out of the restaurant to head home. She reached the end of the block before Damen caught up with her.

When he fell into step beside her, she glanced over at him. "Where are you going?"

"I'm walking you home, or are you catching a bus?"

"That won't be necessary."

"I want to."

She picked up the pace a little. "Do you offer this personal service to all your waitresses at Marquette's?"

He grinned, and the setting sun glinted off his glasses. "No, just to the ones who used to be my lover."

Heaven tripped, and Damen's arm shot out to catch her. "W-what did you say?"

"You heard me, Heaven."

CHAPTER FOUR

Heaven swallowed. She pulled out of Damen's hold and started walking again, keeping her gaze on the sidewalk ahead. He couldn't have said… No, he did say it. He'd said he gave special treatment only to the women who had been his lover. *Okay, Heaven, he could be acting all confident like it's a done deal that he'll sleep with you. Don't jump to conclusions that he remembers the past.*

She lectured herself, but her words didn't ring true, as if that's what Damen had meant. At the same time, she couldn't bring herself to make him clarify. "I was…um…I planned to stop at a small grocery near my place. You don't have to come along. Thanks for walking me this far."

He checked behind them, and she did too like an airhead. They had stridden maybe half a block. Heaven frowned at the man she had seen a few times at the restaurant. He was bigger than the Marquettes but not sexy like them. Rather he appeared rough and liable to take a person's head off. Fear closed her throat, and she stumbled again.

Damen drew her close to his side. "What's wrong, Heaven? I didn't mean to upset you with what I said."

"You didn't." She tried to pull herself together.

Damen's hold tightened. "You're shaking. I told you, I don't want you to be afraid of me."

She looked into his worried gaze, and she reached up about to touch his face but drew back. *Get a grip.* "It's that man. I think he's following us, and I saw him in the restaurant before. No, don't look, Damen. Let's call the police."

He smiled.

"I'm serious!"

"I know, but don't let Guy bother you. He's my bodyguard."

"Bodyguard?"

"Yeah, I'll call him over and introduce him."

"No!"

"Heaven, Guy won't ever hurt you. If I tell him to, he'll protect you, just like he does me."

"Why would you do that?" She shook her head, looking at the man. He still scared her, but she was glad he wasn't some crazy stalker. Rough men, mean ones, got to her, and she steered clear of them. All she wanted now was peace and safety. "I'm fine, Damen. Thanks. Please, just go back."

She broke away from him and walked on. A part of her wanted him to keep pushing, but she breathed a sigh of relief when he didn't. After another block, she glanced back to find Damen and the Guy nowhere in sight. A sense of loneliness came over her, but she hurried along to get home in time to shower and change before she had to pick up Gideon. For the rest of the night and the next morning while at her regular job, Heaven wondered did Damen mean what she thought he did? Did he truly recall her from so long ago?

Twelve years ago.

"'If you ever looked at me once with what I know is in you, I would be your slave.' Do you know what it means?"

Heaven glanced up from the book she held into the most amazing eyes she had ever seen. She couldn't help her gaze wandering over the man, so tall and sexy, if very nerdy with glasses too big and hair cut like he'd just stepped out of the military. When she lingered on the glasses, she bit off a laugh because he snatched them from his face. The poor white boy blushed to the roots of his hair. He'd been leaning against the stacks, trying to strike a cool pose, but it came off as awkward. Her heartbeat kicked up right away.

"Yes, I love Emily Brontë. She's my favorite novelist and poet. You like her too, huh?"

He ran a hand over his hair and shifted from foot to foot. "No, I mean do you know what it means because my instructor is chewing my ass out on this stuff. I hate it."

She gasped. "That's sacrilege, buddy, and seriously the meaning of that passage is elementary."

His face flamed, but he said with boldness, "If I don't pass English, I can't get to my field, and I might have to quit school. I might become a bum begging in the streets, hungry and cold."

She put a hand on her hip. "Are you being funny or dramatic?"

"Both. Do you feel sorry for me?"

"Maybe."

Damen held up a slip of paper, and she leaned closer to decipher the sloppy writing. Her name appeared and where she could be found—haunting the library.

"Why do you have my name?"

"Well, I was hoping it wasn't my friend's idea of a joke as to the woman who could help me with English Lit."

"I'm not a tutor."

"But you get Emily. Heaven, help me."

She laughed, and so did he. The librarian cast them a warning glance, and Heaven grabbed Damen's hand to lead him around several stacks. When they stopped, she faced him.

"I know Emily, but I don't know you."

"Damen Marquette, and if you have any problems with any other subject, I can help you."

She blinked at him. "Any subject?"

He shrugged. "Any one. I can memorize whatever I need to know. I can comprehend complex formulas and procedures. Historical dates stick in my head like glue. Emotional touchy feely stuff is my kryptonite. I don't get it. I don't *want* to get it. So, you help me with Emily, I help you with everything else, and I guarantee to get you an A."

Heaven rolled her eyes. "You think you're all that, huh?"

"I'm a genius."

"Literally?"

"Literally."

"Wow, okay, get me my good grades, Damen, and I'll explain Emily, Chaucer, and any other poets all day and night."

He tugged a lock of her hair, his eyes glazed as if he were mesmerized. "I'll give you whatever you want, Heaven."

Her senses went into a tailspin until he dropped to the floor, groaning and muttering "lame, lame, lame!" Heaven stared down at him and noted his nape flaming red, the color going from the roots of his hair and disappearing beneath his shirt collar. She laughed. Poor man had so little confidence in anything other than his brain, but that's what drew her closer.

Heaven stooped so her lips were close to his ear. "Sounded pretty good to me."

He glanced up and then flashed that one in a million smile. When he stood straight in front of her, his height dwarfed hers, and nerves made her lick dry lips. Damen followed the movement with his gaze.

"He was right," Damen said.

"Who was?"

"My friend."

"What do you mean?"

Damen held the scrap of paper up again but flipped to the other side. She read the words. "Most beautiful nerd, black beauty. Can't miss her."

Heaven frowned. "I'm not sure how I should take that."

"A compliment." Damen leaned in and slanted his mouth over hers. From the moment their lips touched, she was lost, but it was only an instant before he drew back. His eyes were wide behind his glasses. "Sorry. I don't know why I did that."

"Because I wanted you to." She grabbed his shirtfront and stepped closer. Most of the guys at her school were intimidated by her father. If Damen didn't know, and it looked like he didn't—the paper didn't include her last name—she was going to enjoy him for just a little while.

His cock was hard when she pressed against his body, and it bumped her belly. She tilted her head back, inviting his kiss, and Damen didn't hesitate. They kissed and kissed, his tongue snaking into her mouth. Tomorrow he might run off or keep her at a distance, but today, she wrapped her arms around his neck and curved her body to his. Damen encircled her waist and crushed her to his chest. The hungry exploration of each other's mouths didn't stop until somebody cleared their throat, and she sprang away.

Heaven darted down another aisle, but Damen followed like a lost puppy. "Do you always kiss men like that when you first meet them?"

She glared over her shoulder at him. "No, but I won't do it again."

"Too bad."

She peered at him. He was smiling not judging her. Of course he liked it. "You wanted a tutor not a lover."

"I'll take both."

"Nope, too late." She stopped before a section on the Second World War and selected a book at random. Damen's fingers touched hers and traced over her hand to her wrist. Long fingers circled around and tugged gently. She almost dropped the book but transferred it to the other hand. He didn't let go, but he didn't push too much either. Their fingers laced together.

"I know I'm awkward," he said. "But I don't think I'm too bad to look at."

She eyed him. "You a'ight."

He chuckled. "So do you have any problem with my skin color?"

"No, of course not. Why would I?"

"Just checking." He released her hand and stroked her cheek. Heaven leaned into it before she realized what she was doing. Then she spun away, putting her back to him. Way too intimate for a first meeting, but she was always like that. Not the kissing part, but the hope inside when they touched her. *Damn, damn, damn!*

She had seriously crossed the line with Damen, maybe

because of his awkwardness and the gentle look in his eyes.

"Okay," Damen said behind her. "Let's keep it professional. You help me. I help you. That's all. Sound good?"

She faced him. "Yeah, sounds good."

He nodded and stuck his hand out. "We'll start over. Damen Marquette, genius idiot."

"Heaven… Nerd."

"*Beautiful* nerd. Get it right."

"Oh yeah, I forgot."

Heaven crossed over to Saint Louis Street and started walking. Halfway to Marquette's, she spotted a familiar face up ahead and came to a stop. Damen leaned against a wall, hands in his pockets and whistling as if he always spent his late afternoons hanging in the street. She hesitated and scanned the area, but she didn't spot Guy anywhere.

"What are you doing, Damen?" she demanded when she drew up alongside him.

He shrugged. "Enjoying the weather."

"It's hot."

"Are you saying I look sweaty?"

Let's be real. Even if you did, you'd look good enough to eat. She said none of this out loud to the big-headed man. "No, I'm saying, you aren't just hanging around here for no reason. You were waiting for me."

He smiled. "You're pretty sure of yourself."

"I'm not!" She grumbled. "Don't play with me, Damen. I'm not in the mood. You didn't come by my house, did you? I won't be stalked."

He grew serious. "Of course not. I wouldn't do that

unless you invited me. I also don't know your address. Creed handles personnel files, and while I could get into them, I'm not going to violate your privacy. I know the general direction you come from, and yes, I was waiting for you."

She kept walking, and he fell into step beside her. "Why, and where is your bodyguard? Shouldn't he keep watching over you just in case? I know all of your faces have been in the media so many times. Everyone knows who you are."

"Are you worried about me, beautiful?"

She rolled her eyes at him.

"He's around. I told him to stay out of sight because he frightens you."

"I'm not scared of him," she lied, but it surprised her he would go to such lengths on her behalf. "I don't want you to risk your safety for me."

"I'm not. Don't worry. Guy's keeping watch from wherever he is."

She looked around again but was kind of too scared to spot him, so she let it go. "You still haven't told me why you're following me around like a lost puppy."

If she expected him to blush like he did in the past, she was doomed to wait forever. He hitched his shoulders and stuffed his hands into his pockets again. Heaven tried looking away from him, but she couldn't make her eyes obey. Just a little longer. He must have shaved a second time that day because even with it being late afternoon, his jaw was smooth. He smelled like sandalwood.

"Heaven, I don't think you forgot our sessions," he said. "In New York."

Well, that cleared that up. "The hours we spent studying."

"The hours spent *not* studying," he corrected.

She bit her lip. "I remember you, but it was a long time

46

ago."

He agreed.

"You didn't remember me when I first came to Marquette's." She could kick herself for bringing that up. Her words sounded whiny and self-pitying.

"I remembered as soon as I saw your face. I thought I would prompt you by saying your name was familiar." His gaze swept her body, and Heaven hoped the tightening of her nipples wasn't noticeable through her bra and work clothes. Damen's lingering look made her wonder.

"Oh well, whatever." She waved her hand. "What's in the past is past. Not a big deal now. I heard you got married and…" She trailed off because she couldn't bring herself to introduce the subject of his daughter. If she did, that left her open to discuss Gideon. Not taking the cues would mean she was truly lying to him, and she couldn't come down to that. The problem was, if she didn't discuss the little girl, she couldn't gauge what kind of dad he was. Even her dad came off warm and wonderful to everyone else.

"Yes, I was married."

Heaven started at the tone of Damen's voice. He always sounded open and friendly, but at the mention of his ex-wife, he closed off like a vault. She had been worried the conversation would turn to the kids, but they seemed to be the farthest from his mind.

"I'm sorry if I brought up something painful."

He rolled his shoulders, and this time she knew it was to release the tension. "No, it's fine. I loved her."

Heaven refused to identify the twinge in her own chest.

"Vida wasn't right for me."

The world dipped and bobbed around Heaven, but she sucked in a deep breath, slowing her gait. Damen fell back to match her step, and she worked hard not to let him notice how his words affected her. She wanted to change the subject because she hadn't expected him to even share about his ex-wife with her. No other topic came to her befuddled mind.

"I'm sorry," she said lamely.

"I thought she was like us."

"Like us? You mean more in love with books than anything else?"

He gave a sheepish grin. "The way I used to be, yes."

Used to be. Now he was like a social butterfly.

"I was content to live a quiet, comfortable life back then, most nights spent at home with an occasional visit to a cultural event or the museum. A movie or two wasn't so bad."

"Wow, when you put it like that, I guess it does sound dry." Heaven tried to think of the last time she went out and did something crazy just to have fun. She couldn't recall, but then her life had been controlled, except for when it came to Gideon. If Gideon wanted to watch a movie, she took him. Almost anything he wanted, she was there. Now, though, her son seemed to stretch his wings a bit more and was doing more on his own, like the self-defense classes and the sports. He'd never been interested in that. In a weird way, he was behaving like Damen without the two of them knowing each other.

"Yeah." Damen scowled.

"I didn't mean you're boring, Damen. You don't come off that way to me at all. I don't know what you do in your private time, but you seem radically different from the way you were years ago."

He stopped walking, and she felt obliged to as well. "Heaven, are you still attracted to me?"

"W-wah?" she croaked.

"Are you?" He stepped closer. "I want you to be honest."

She swallowed and weighed the options. "You're a sexy man, but you knew that."

"Meaning intellectually, you're turned off."

She laughed. "No, for all I know you've dumped Tolstoy for the latest football stats or something like that."

His smirk made butterflies stir in her belly. "I was never into Tolstoy."

"So kidding."

He moved even nearer, stealing her breath. "In my private time, I create apps for android phones."

"For fun?"

He shrugged. "I also rock climb, go jet skiing, and invest in failing businesses just to see if I can turn them around. I think I might try sky diving sometime."

"The rumors were true."

"Yes."

"You really rock climb?" She was in awe.

"Heaven, you haven't answered my question."

"I said you're sexy."

He waited in silence.

"All right. Yes, I'm still attracted to you. That makes no difference because I…" She had been about to say getting involved with him wasn't why she was there. He wasn't even asking her the crucial question of what the heck she was doing working as a waitress. Then again, he might think she was doing what he did, some radical lifestyle outside of their norm just to see what it was like. Did he think she would disappear soon when the novelty wore off? Probably so.

"Then let's have an affair."

"What?" She screeched too loud and looked around to

see if other people on the street had noticed. Several looked their way, and she cleared her throat, embarrassed. "You're not serious."

Damen ran a finger along her jawline, sending chills racing up and down her spine. "I'm very serious. When you left all those years ago, I wasn't done with you. I wanted more of you, but you disappeared. Since we had agreed we were just having a little fun, I let you go. It was obvious your fun was over."

She tried to think of a response. The best course was to agree, but the truth was that's when her father had sent her away to have the baby. He had grudgingly footed the bill, but as soon as she could, Heaven had gotten onto her own two feet and had taken care of her and Gideon ever since.

"As you said," Damen continued, "we're different people now. We've had more experiences, and I'm curious to see how it will translate with the two of us in bed."

Them in bed, Heaven thought, and her body came to life. Her panties were wet, no doubt about it, with just the suggestion of his hands touching her skin. Yet, Damen still loved his ex. She could see that, and she was fresh from leaving hers. Sure, she wasn't stupid enough not to use protection this time, but meeting Damen wasn't about her.

Not to mention, her body had changed. She maintained a small size by reason of the abuse. That wasn't the case now, but she had had a baby. Her belly was covered in stretchmarks, her pussy probably not as tight as it had been at age twenty. Hell, nobody's was even without a baby after so many years. Even so, the physical changes weren't what scared her.

The fear came from this man, Damen. Would he be a tender lover as he had been then, or did that part change too, and he was rougher? More experience didn't translate into being good or caring about the satisfaction of one's partner. Damen came off as a man whose chief concern was getting his, and she had to wonder how many of the waitresses had been in his bed.

Heaven spun away and started walking again. "I don't think so, Damen. You're going to have to let this one get away. Creed said—"

She slapped a hand over her mouth. Damen frowned. "What did my brother say?"

"Nothing."

"Don't lie to me, Heaven."

She kept walking, but he grabbed her arm. She didn't mean to cry out, and Damen's eyes widened in shock when she raised her other hand to block a blow. Breaking free, she started to run, but Damen passed her in a couple long strides. He didn't even have to break into a run. He obstructed her path, but he didn't attempt to touch her again.

"Someone hurt you, Heaven."

"No."

"You're lying again." He didn't sound angry this time, at least not at her. When she had a moment to calm down, she realized his grasp on her arm hadn't even hurt, and he hadn't been about to hit her. The reaction was automatic, and she kicked herself for letting him see it.

She raised her chin and looked him in the eyes. "Whatever happened in my life is my business. You said earlier you wouldn't violate my privacy."

He seemed disappointed, but he nodded. "I won't."

"Good. Please, let it go, okay? It's in the past."

"Promise me it *is* in the past, and I won't bring it up again."

She didn't answer fast enough.

"Heaven!"

"It is." Then she smiled, remembering their new start. "We...*I* am free, and no one is going to hurt me ever again."

She thought of her dad and decided in that moment she wouldn't see him either. Not that he ever touched her, but he knew how to hurt her feelings. She was cutting him off too, and with so many miles between them, it was easy. A new calm came over her.

Damen must have sensed it. "I'm glad. No wonder you were afraid of Guy. I'll keep him out of sight from now on."

"You don't have to do that."

"I want you to feel safe while you're at Marquette's for as long as you're there."

His words confirmed what he thought she was doing, giving waitressing a try for the heck of it. Hell, if she was going to *try* something, it wouldn't be standing on her damn feet all day. She'd let him believe that for the time being.

They started toward the restaurant again.

"Heaven, what did Creed say?"

She sighed. "You're not going to drop it, are you?"

"I could ask him."

"Fine. He said you're not serious, and you won't cross the line, so basically, don't get any stupid ideas."

Damen laughed. "And I make him wrong by asking you to be my lover."

"You're saying you haven't slept with every waitress there?"

"Of course not. What do you think we're running?"

"You like to flirt."

"It's just something to do. How about this, if you agree to be my lover, I won't flirt with any other woman but you."

She found herself panting. Stupid idiot shouldn't say

stuff like that. "That's feeding right into Creed's warning about getting ideas."

"Hm." He rubbed his jaw as if he considered it, but there was a twinkle in the fool's eyes that she didn't like. "I suppose so. You are a woman, a beautiful one, but still a woman."

Heaven cut her eyes at him. "Thanks."

"Can't be helped," he grumbled. "I want you, and I can't turn it off. So, we can do it like last time. Any time you want to disappear, just go."

She gaped at him. "Damen, are you serious?"

He blocked her path and leaned so close, his breath warmed her lips. "I'll give you whatever you want, Heaven."

CHAPTER FIVE

"Damen, what are you doing?"

"Fuck off, big bro." Damen popped a grape into his mouth and leaned back in his chair. Light construction had begun in his new office, but for the time being, he shared space with Creed in his. Damen didn't care because he never sat still for long. His duties kept him serving, seating, and schmoozing their guests. He didn't mind that part of his job either, so long as he got time to go off on his own and disappear from the world.

"Damen!" Creed jerked his shirtfront and forced Damen forward. Damen ground his teeth and narrowed his eyes at his brother. Right away, Creed released him. Damen, more than his brothers, hated violence. Creed knew that and apologized. "Why are you going after her? You don't usually do more than flirt with the waitresses. They know it, so I don't bug you. This one is different. Is it because she's black, because of Shada?"

Damen wrinkled his brow. "What does your woman have to do with anything?"

"Jealousy."

Damen laughed. "No, you've got your own problems with that one."

"The two of you never liked each other."

"I don't dislike her. She's going to be my sister-in-law as soon as you convince her to stop running from you."

His oldest brother grumbled in annoyance, but he didn't deny the truth. Creed had taken to calling Shada his fiancée to everyone and within hearing distance of Shada. She'd said yes, but so far, she wouldn't set a date. Talk about being backward. Men were notorious for skirting commitment. His brother was all for it, but Shada's past kept her digging her heels in. Damen wondered who would win in the end, him or her.

"Good luck breaking down those walls, bro."

"This isn't about me," Creed snapped.

"Hey, you're the one that brought up Shada." Damen was matter-of-fact with the conversation so far, but Heaven came to mind. He wanted her. Back in college, he'd enjoyed every time they had sex. Her body was incredible and her responses to his touch so sensual. Even while he had loved his ex-wife she had never responded to him the way Heaven had. Would it be the same, or worse? Maybe better.

Thinking of Heaven, his cock swelled in his pants, and he leaned forward to slide up to his desk. Good thing he was on break. He had to get control of this hard-on before he scared the old ladies that dined with them on an almost nightly basis.

"Damen, are you listening?"

"Yeah." He hadn't been.

"It's becoming obvious that you can't take your eyes off her. I've had complaints."

That got Damen's attention. "Who complained?"

Creed hesitated. Had Heaven gone to Creed? The last thing he wanted to do was frighten her. She'd said she wasn't afraid of him, but she could have been lying. He had seen the way she reacted thinking he would hit her, and it had ignited a rage in him that probably rivaled Creed's anger. There was also the instance when she first spotted Guy. She might have smooth chocolate skin, but she had gone pale and shook so hard he thought she would faint. Who had dared to make her that scared?

"Who?" Damen repeated. "Was it Heaven?"

Creed appeared surprised. "I doubt any woman you set your sights on will turn you down."

"Heaven is different."

"Oh, is it love?"

Damen scoffed. "Don't be ridiculous. Love doesn't exist."

"Just leave her alone, Damen. Let her do her job. She's obviously been through something, or she wouldn't be here."

Damen considered telling Creed about their past together but dismissed it. He had a feeling it would make no difference one way or another. Heaven wasn't working tonight, and he wished she was. At least her round ass and perfect breasts gave him something to look at. Despite what his brother told him, he knew he wasn't being obvious about staring at Heaven. The only way anyone would know was if they were staring an inordinate amount at him. Tiff came to mind, and he sighed. He shouldn't have flirted so much with her after Marisa, his brief lover and Shada's sister, had passed away.

Damen pushed fingers through his hair and shut his eyes. He ran through the mental exercise he'd given to Heaven but with a few modifications. After some time, his hard-on eased, and he rearranged his cock.

Music started up in the main dining room, and he knew it was Stefan playing rather than the man they had hired to entertain at night. His youngest brother couldn't get enough of music, and in truth, neither could he. Music soothed the savage beast—Creed—and it helped Damen's temperament too. He chuckled to himself at his silent joke at his brother's expense.

He pushed back his chair and stood. "I'm going out there and joining him."

"You're singing tonight?" Creed asked.

Damen grinned. "Relax. We won't rope you into anything."

"As if you could."

"All it takes is a bug in Shada's ear." Damen let out a bark of laughter at the anger in Creed's eyes. He loved ribbing Creed. "Creed, you're easy."

"Shut the hell up, and get out so I can get some work done."

Damen hummed the tune his brother played as he left the office. When he pushed through the kitchen door into the dining room, he spied the kid that had come by not long ago. He had disappeared, but now he stood against a wall, eyes wide, pulling ear buds from his ears. Damen followed his line of sight and found him staring at Stefan as his fingers danced over the piano keys.

"Another music lover," he said and shook his head as he weaved through the tables toward the boy. "Ah, I see you're back. Couldn't stay away?"

The boy looked up at him with wide, brown eyes, desperate eyes, Damen thought. He had a flashback to his and his brothers' early days when they were teens. So many days were spent hungry, so many with the same worn clothing and sometimes bills unpaid so the electricity was out.

At least the boy had ditched the ratty jacket. He didn't wear one tonight, but that might have something to do with the heat. Damen didn't want to jump to conclusions about this kid or every kid he came across for that matter. He and Stefan had discussed with Creed about starting a foundation for kids that were in the same boat they had been in all those years ago. Maybe with the project on his mind, he was projecting need onto this boy. Well, either way, he wouldn't turn him away no matter what.

"I'm not hungry," the boy said, and Damen chuckled.

"Okay."

"But…" The boy shuffled from one foot to the other and ducked his head. "Can I stay?"

Damen scoured his memory for the boy's name. What was it again? While he thought, the boy seemed to assume his answer was no and turned to go. Damen called out after him. "Gideon."

Sunshine seemed to break out on the small face. His eyebrows rose. "You remembered my name!"

"Of course. We're friends now, right? Come on. Why don't you move closer?" Damen pointed. "I happen to know there's a spot right there beside the piano that's available."

Gideon gasped. "No way. I'd get in trouble."

"With who?" Damen wrapped an arm about the thin shoulders and drew Gideon to his side. "You forgot I'm one of the bosses."

When Damen had Gideon settled, he strode over to Stefan, and they nodded to each other. Damen bent to remove his guitar from the case and plugged it into the amp.

He set a few of the dials and tested the strings to get the sound where he wanted. A quick run over the scale, and he shut his eyes a moment to feel the music. So satisfying.

Damen didn't have a desire to go pro. He never did, and he knew his skill was mediocre at best, but playing with Stefan just gave him that extra thing he needed. Just like getting lost in a good book fed his soul, so did music and rock climbing. Creed got onto him sometimes about changing himself to meet what he thought a woman would want. He had said Damen ran after Stefan to appear to be the impulsive, fun type of man. Maybe that was true in the beginning, and in some respects it might still be true. He knew he had unresolved issues. Regardless, he had freed his soul too, allowed himself to be anything, and he wouldn't change back for Creed or any woman.

Stefan gave the signal, and Damen stirred from his reverie. He and his brother sang, harmonizing with ease. Damen glanced over at Gideon to find the boy staring at him this time. He winked, and the kid blushed. Damen chuckled. Cute kid. He'd better not find out someone was neglecting him.

For a straight hour, Damen and Stefan played, and Damen met the gazes of several women dining tonight that met his interest. Normally, he would choose one and meet her later for drinks, except he was holding out that Heaven changed her mind. Perhaps he needed to step up his seduction. Yeah, that's exactly what he would do later.

When the performance ended, Damen crouched to lock his guitar away. Before he could shut the case, a pair of sneakers appeared beside him, and a small, hesitant voice asked, "Can I touch it? I promise, I won't break it."

Damen glanced up at Gideon and then to his brother.

"Hey, Stefan, why don't you distract the ladies for me for a while."

"Sure." Stefan rubbed his hands together as if ready to feast, but Damen knew he was joking. He assumed his youngest brother had lovers, but he had never seen any, nor did Stefan ever favor any of their younger guests.

Damen shook his head at the man and pulled the guitar out of the case. "Slide that chair over here, Gideon."

The boy complied, and when he was seated, Damen placed the guitar in his arms. Gideon's eyes bugged. "Are you sure?"

"Why not? It's just an instrument. If you damage it, it can be repaired. Besides, it's not that delicate. Go for it."

Gideon's chin dropped to his chest as he maneuvered long, slim fingers. Well, he had the hands for it if nothing else. Damen winced at the discordant sound and moved behind the boy. He leaned over the small frame and placed his hands over Gideon's. Gently, he began to show him, sliding the boy's fingers up and down the strings, placing pressure when needed. He marveled at the fact that Gideon completely gave into him and let him lead him. The music, although still not perfect, flowed enough for both of them to enjoy. Damen leaned to the side a little more so he could see Gideon's face. The boy had shut his eyes, mouth agape.

"You really love music, huh?" Damen asked.

Gideon snapped out of it and jumped to his feet. He shoved the guitar at Damen. "I guess."

"You want to be a musician when you grow up?" Damen knew some kids dreamed of it. For a while, Stefan was determined to follow that path. Creed and Damen never tried to talk him out of it, but they had hoped he would let it go. Their dad had been a musician by trade, a poor one, because he drank up any profits and ruined opportunities by getting into fights while drunk. Damen was glad his daughter Nita hadn't inherited their love of music, at least not so far, and if he had his way, she never would.

"I don't know," Gideon said. "I just like it a lot. I never thought about playing any instruments."

Damen wondered if had he inadvertently introduced the kid to new ideas in that direction? "Well, you're only what, nine?" He guessed low on purpose to see the kid's reaction.

Gideon frowned and clenched his hands into fists. "I'm eleven!"

Damen chuckled. "My mistake. I apologize."

"Sorry." Gideon ducked his head and shuffled his feet. "I'm kind of short for my age. Everybody in my class is always taller."

"Hm, most likely your growth spurt hasn't happened yet."

Gideon rolled his eyes. "That's what my mom keeps telling me. I think it's just what grown-ups tell short kids to make them feel better."

Damen laughed. "Okay, how about some science?"

"Huh?"

"How tall is your mom?"

Gideon told him, and Damen nodded.

"Okay, how about your dad?"

The boy hesitated, and Damen kicked himself. Maybe he didn't know or had never met the man. Then Gideon got a funny look on his face. "Your height."

"Great. I'm six feet. So, the formula goes like this—to predict a boy's height you add five inches to his mother's height and add that to his father's height. The total is then divided by two. Can you come up with the number?"

"I'm uh…do you have any paper?" Gideon said.

Damen didn't know if Gideon was too nervous to calculate in his head or unsure of the formula. He ran down the figures as he counted them in his head. "So basically, we can predict that you'll be about six feet tall when you grow up. There's no guarantee of course. It could go up or down by a couple inches, but you'll probably be close to that. What do you think? Sound good?"

Gideon's mouth fell open. "You didn't make that up, did you?"

Damen grinned. "No. I collect a lot of useless facts up here." He tapped the side of his head. "But in your case, it came in handy."

"I always have a hard time in school. I can barely pass my classes, and my mom has to put me in tutoring every year. I hate it. I hate being stupid. I wish I was smart like you."

"Easy, partner." Damen squeezed his shoulder. "You're not dumb."

"Tell that to my grades."

Damen scratched his head. He had zero idea how to make Gideon feel better about himself or how to encourage him. The height thing came easy because he had studied up on it for no other reason than it was something to do. That was a hobby of his, right up there with getting a Ph.D. in Forensics for the hell of it.

Most subjects came easily to him. Studying wasn't something he needed to make a habit of in school. He just retained most everything, except when it came to English Lit, and he had had Heaven for that. Being a man who never had to struggle with school, how the hell could he give Gideon advice?

"Well, uh…" he began, fumbling.

"It doesn't matter. Da— Uh…"

"It's fine. You can call me Damen if you want."

The boy looked taken aback. Maybe his mother was strict about respecting adults.

"Or whatever you like," he amended quickly.

"Can I come again?"

Damen glanced toward the doors and noted the sun had gone down. "Of course you can, as often as you want, but you need to get your mother's permission. It's getting late. You shouldn't be out there alone. I'll walk you home."

"No!"

Damen's brows rose.

"I mean I'm not a little kid. I can get home by myself, and I live close by."

Damen hesitated. He rubbed his jaw and then had an idea. "Okay, that's fine. I'll see you again, okay? Maybe we can talk some more, and heck, I'm sure I could convince Stefan to teach you a little on piano. I don't play it."

Gideon glanced over at the piano and back at him. "Is it all right if I play with you instead?"

"Sure, bud."

The bright smile flashed, one Damen was starting to like. He touched the top of the kid's head and watched as he headed out. Damen made a hand signal, and Guy came into view from wherever he had been. A nod toward the boy sent his bodyguard into motion, and he slipped out the front door after Gideon.

CHAPTER SIX

Heaven stood before the crate of tomatoes and counted out the number needed in the kitchen. She was helping out back here for the next couple of hours, and she didn't mind. The break from serving tables meant she could avoid fighting to keep her eyes off Damen for a while. The man seemed always to be on duty when she was. She shouldn't complain, because this was what she wanted, to see what Damen was truly like. The problem came in when fatherhood was the farthest thing from her mind, and all she thought of was sleeping with him.

Heaven already knew she was two seconds from accepting his offer to become lovers again. Nervousness and fear had faded, and desire took over. One more time, her idiot mind kept telling her. Just sleep with him once after so long, and everything would be okay.

Yeah, right. She couldn't believe it, but after the idea presented itself she couldn't dismiss it either. Annoyed at herself, she started out of the larder but froze when angry voices reached her from the hall.

"We need to talk," Creed snapped. "In my office."

"I'm busy, Creed, and don't you want our guests to eat when they get here?"

"Don't give me that attitude, Shada. You've been putting me off for weeks."

"Well, the restaurant is not the place to do it."

"It is when you leave our bed at the crack of dawn to avoid me!"

Heaven winced. She moved over to the door and eased it wider. There was no squeak from rusty hinges, of course. The Marquettes ran a tight ship, but knowing it didn't stop her nerves.

Heaven had just gotten the door wide enough to slip out, planning to escape into the kitchen in case Creed and Shada came her way and thought she purposely eavesdropped. Before she could clear the door, a bulky figure pressed her backward and pushed the door almost shut. She thrust at Damen's chest with no result whatsoever.

"Move, Damen," she whispered. "I was just about to get out of here."

"Too late. They're right outside."

She didn't believe him, but it did seem like Creed and Shada's voices had grown louder. Heaven maneuvered around Damen to face the door, but he stood so close behind her, she felt the heat off his body. He crowded her on purpose, the bum. The larder was plenty big enough for the both of them. Damen's hands came down on her shoulders, and he squeezed. Her ridiculous body behaved as if he had rubbed a hand between her legs. To try to regain control of herself, she focused on the arguing couple.

"Nobody's avoiding you, Creed. Stop being dramatic."

"So you're being completely honest with me?" he demanded.

"Yes!"

"Then what's this?"

Everything went quiet. Heaven would kill to see what he showed her.

"I-I-I," she stuttered.

Heaven looked over her shoulder at Damen. He shrugged, but then his gaze shifted to her lips. She swiveled her head back to face the door.

"You don't understand." Shada's voice was almost too quiet to hear.

Now, Creed wasn't yelling either. "No, I don't. You agreed to marry me, and you said we could try for a baby. I didn't push you into it. Now I find out you were back on the pill without telling me."

Heaven slapped a hand over her mouth, and Damen cursed.

"Creed," Shada cried.

"Fuck it, Shada. I'm done."

"What's that supposed to mean?"

"*We're* done. I can't fight your fear. I'm not going to anymore."

Running steps in the hall reached Heaven, a door slam, and then Stefan's voice. "Creed, wait a sec. Where are you going?"

Heaven looked up at Damen again. "You should go after your brother."

"No."

She spun to face him. "Don't you care?"

"Of course I do."

"Then, why don't you talk to him? He must be hurting."

"I'm sure he is, but…"

"But what, Damen?" She put her hands on her hips, waiting for him to give her a good explanation.

"He didn't want me to tell anyone."

"Tell them what?"

He grunted and leaned against a shelf, folding his arms over his chest and crossing his legs at the ankles. "Damn, he's stubborn. He didn't even want me to tell Stefan, but I don't blame him for that. Knowing my youngest brother, he would have blabbed the truth to Shada so she wouldn't be hurt."

Heaven's eyes widened. "Are you saying he's been cheating with someone else? I find that impossible to believe."

Damen smirked, but she thought she saw a spark of annoyance. "Are you into my brother?"

"Of course not. I'm just pretty sure Creed is crazy about Shada, and honestly, if they can't work it out, then what hope is there for the rest of us?"

"True." Damen extended a hand and dragged Heaven closer. She stumbled over his feet and fell against his chest. His arms encircled her, trapping her in place. "That's why relationships are not the answer. The answer is in mutual satisfaction."

"Damen, let me go. The kitchen staff is expecting this food."

"The one you were collecting it for is Shada. Am I right?"

She glared at him.

"I'm guessing she's not in the mood to cook anything right now, so no one needs the tomatoes."

"Have you always been this cold, and I wasn't aware of it?" She fought to get free. His fingertips traced along her spine, and she shivered. Thank goodness he stopped just above her butt, but it was far too late for her panties either way. Her pussy was practically begging for his attention.

"I'm not cold," he whispered, bringing his lips close to her throat. "Just realistic."

"Damen, let me go."

"I don't want to." He kissed her skin right where her pulse raced. "Let me make love to you tonight."

Her fingers curled into his shirtsleeves. He moved his mouth from her throat to her lips, but just touching. If he thought she would open to him, he could wait forever. Heaven shut her eyes, struggling against her own desire. *Damn it, why does he have to smell so good and feel so good? It's not fair.*

Heaven managed to turn her head.

"Are you mad at me?" he asked.

She didn't answer, and he sighed.

"Creed found the pills yesterday. We talked about it. He wanted to break it off with her to force her to see that what she wants more than anything is family."

"That's his logic?"

Damen shrugged. "He's an idiot. They broke up at the beginning. It didn't work then, and it's not going to work now."

"He'll end up hurting her."

"My brother is obsessed with Shada. He's not going to let her get away, so don't worry about it. What you should worry about is when he's fighting with her he's evil incarnate."

"Are you exaggerating?"

"Nope."

Heaven began to shake, and Damen cursed. He hugged her tighter.

"Hey, I was joking. I'm sorry. That was in poor taste. Shh, Heaven, baby, he would never hurt you."

She tried to escape him, but he wouldn't let go until she calmed down. When she stopped shaking, and the fear ebbed, Damen captured her lips in the gentlest kiss she had ever experienced. He didn't force his tongue into her mouth but teased her lips in slow, sweet caresses that undid her defenses. He stroked her back, not venturing to her butt, but comforting and igniting passion at the same time.

Heaven lost track of the outside world as she raised her chin higher and accepted Damen's kiss. She parted her lips and invited his tongue in. He baited the tip of her tongue with the tip of his, and she explored deeper into his mouth. He moaned against her lips and drew her higher into his embrace. His erection went from her belly to pressing between her legs, and she cried out in need. The next instant, she found herself on her feet, free of his hold.

Damen walked away a few steps, running his hands through his hair. Heaven liked how he disordered it, and wanted to mess it up some more. *Preferably with him on top of me.*

She almost moaned a second time but suppressed it. "I need to get back out there."

Her feet didn't move, and he didn't say anything. She licked her lips and turned toward the door.

"Heaven."

"Yes?"

"Let me make love to you."

She chewed her bottom lip and then released it. "Okay."

"I'll pick you up—"

"No."

He made no sound when he moved up behind her, but she felt him there.

"We'll work out a schedule, and I'll let you know. Okay?

Please, that's the only way I can accept it right now."

"I don't like waiting for a woman to call."

She spun to face him, grinning. "Well, get over it. Women have been doing it forever. Plus, I'm worth it."

"Yes, you are."

"Good." She kissed her fingers and pressed them dramatically to his lips then left the larder with a flourish. She must be outside her mind, she'd done it. She had agreed to be Damen's lover. This time, she would protect her heart.

"We could have gone to my house," Damen said.

Heaven thought he sounded a little annoyed, but she put it down to him hating that she was calling the shots. Well, he hadn't said no so far. She moved ahead of him into the hotel room after he used the key card to get in. The jazz singer in the lobby eight floors below and the ding of the glass elevator moving from floor to floor muffled to nothing when the door closed.

"You said you would give me anything."

"True, but this feels somewhat impersonal."

"Are you a woman, Damen?"

He frowned.

She fell onto the bed and kicked her shoes off. The softness of the mattress made her lie back and stretch while moaning. Right away, the side of the bed sank with Damen's weight. He leaned over her, his gaze intense as he stared.

"Should I prove I'm not?" he asked.

"The thing on my thigh proves it."

"That could be any*thing.*"

"Well, you could show it to me, I guess. I can pass judgment after."

"Judgment!"

She laughed.

"Heaven."

She heard the seriousness in his tone. He stroked her cheek with the backs of his knuckles, and she couldn't help leaning into his touch. Flutters stirred in her belly, and her pussy clenched with anticipation.

"Is it okay, Heaven?"

She didn't understand. "Is what okay?"

"I want to take your clothes off and make love to you. You need to know I won't hurt you. I'll be gentle."

He was killing her. Tears pricked her eyes, and she blinked until the feeling went away. For a minute, she considered if it was all right. For a long time, she'd hesitated to remove her jacket at work, trying to recall whether there were bruises anyone would notice on her arms. She had been in New Orleans long enough for any and all bruises to fade.

Heaven moved as if she wanted to sit up, and Damen rolled away. She sat on the side of the bed and began unbuttoning her blouse. Today was too hot to wear a jacket, so her arms were already bare. She'd been proud of herself for wearing a short-sleeved blouse.

When the buttons were all undone, she pushed the material over her shoulders and down her arms. The new white lacy bra was sexy against her cinnamon skin, and she noticed her nipples had hardened to the point that they were obvious behind the barrier. Her boobs weren't that big, but they were okay. She was a bit smaller than she wanted to be, even more so than she was all those years ago. Living free had started taking care of that already.

"Touch me, Damen," she said. "I've wanted it for a long time."

He slid closer and helped her remove the blouse the rest of the way then tossed it onto a nearby chair. A hand sliding along her hip, he found the button at the back of her skirt and pinched it open. When Heaven heard the zipper lower, she shivered. Damen stilled.

She leaned toward him and nibbled his bottom lip. "Don't be so scared to hurt me. I'm not that delicate."

"I know you're strong." He caressed her mouth with the pad of a thumb and tipped her chin up. His mouth slanted over hers made her pant and cling to him. Damen tasted good too. He could be a drug if she let him, but she had already told herself, this was temporary. Okay, she had already upped the one time thing to three times, but she drew the line there. Of course, that was dependent on if they enjoyed themselves.

Heaven drew back and pulled his glasses off his face. His eyes mesmerized her to the point that she forgot what she was doing. He took them from her hand and laid them on the bedside table. She came to herself and began unbuttoning his shirt. Was his body the same?

Yes!

Muscular, tanned, beautiful, he made her mouth water. She ran her hands over his chest and plucked at his small, flat nipples. Damen's sharp intake of breath brought an answering one from her. She leaned in to lick his skin, loving the saltiness and the heat. Moaning, she kissed her way from his chest to his throat and explored all around the base of his neck. At his chin, she brushed her nose along there and luxuriated in the smoothness of his skin and the scent of his aftershave.

Damen removed her bra, and he made sure his hands were right there to capture her breasts as they tumbled out. "Hell, yes."

He laid her back on the bed and removed her skirt. Now all she wore were panties and nothing else. Her belly was exposed and her slender limbs. His gaze raked her a moment, and then he took her panties off. She chewed on her bottom lip. Once he had tossed everything aside, his attention was back on her naked body, and he inched her legs apart a little. She felt her wet pussy opening to him.

"You're thinner than before," he commented.

"I—"

"Shh. So damn beautiful, Heaven." He bent low toward her core and kissed her bud. She trembled, and he looked up at her. "Are you nervous?"

"No, Damen, I told you. I've never been afraid of you, and the way you're so careful makes me know I'm right to feel that way. I want to make you feel good too."

"I haven't begun to pleasure you," he said, "but you've already started with me. I'm about to burst right here. Looking at you… Your skin is incredible, your sweet smell. I remember how you taste too."

Her eyes widened. "You do not."

"Like honey." He dipped low and licked along her slit. She yelped in pleasure, and he sat up grinning. "See? Delicious."

"Whatever."

He climbed off the bed and stood between her legs. Heaven sat up quickly to brush his hands away from his pants. She wanted to do it, and he let her. When the button was open, she lowered the zipper, her entire being strained to see his cock. Damen didn't need judging. She remembered him too, that his dick was thick and long, and best of all that he took his time with it to please them both.

Pushing his pants and boxers down at the same time, Heaven got a face full of his big cock, and kissed the tip.

Damen moaned and pushed fingers into her hair. "You don't have to do that."

She ignored him and sucked his cock between her lips. If they had never been together and she didn't know him well, she wouldn't have done it the first time. This was Damen, and she already knew how much she enjoyed tasting the throbbing length, how he made those strangled noises in the back of his throat and how he struggled to hold on and not come too fast.

"Ah, Heaven, your mouth, baby. You're killing me."

She knew she was as she took him deep into her throat, sucked hard, and let him slide out. Pumping his erection from base to just under the head, she knew what he liked. Heaven licked the head and pulled it between her lips, and then she let it pop from her mouth to look up at him.

"Do you still like it like this?"

"Yes, but let me eat you, baby. I want to hear the sounds you make."

"Not until I'm finished."

Damen's hand dropped onto her shoulder. She thought he would push her back to make her stop, but he seemed to lose all strength. He hissed between his teeth, and she felt his balls growing tighter already. Satisfied that she had full control of this sexy man, she worked him until he barked a warning, one that meant nothing to her because she drank his come without a second thought.

Heaven raised her head afterward, smirking at Damen. "You bum, you expected it."

"I didn't."

"Pineapples."

"I might have eaten one or two."

She laughed. They had both learned he could flavor his

come with what he ate, and she had enjoyed the taste of pineapples. Heaven kissed the tip of his cock again. "Just for that…"

He leaned down and raised her up from the side of the bed to rest her in the center. His shoulder nudged her legs apart. "Just for that I'm going to enjoy my favorite honey."

"Damen."

He locked onto her clit, and she came up off the bed. Pleasure fired along her veins and stirred her core muscles. She whimpered and grasped both sides of his head as he sucked her bud into his mouth. Heaven rode his face, pumping against it. She cried out his name and teetered too soon onto an orgasm.

"No, please, not yet."

She worried for an instant he might think she wanted him to stop, but Damen knew her body. He stuck a finger carefully into her heat and wiggled it while he used the tip of his tongue to flick her clit. She bit off a scream, but there was no stopping the climax. The powerful sensations crashed over her, sweeping her along. Wave after wave swept through her, and she was left at the mercy of Damen's tongue. Just when she grew sensitive to the touch, he raised his head and kissed along her thighs.

"Damen."

He looked at her. "Feel good?"

"Yes, so good."

"There's more where that came from."

"I want you in me, please."

"I'm not hard yet."

"Can I help you?"

He moved up the bed to lie beside her, and they stared into each other's eyes. Damen flattened a palm against her mouth. She grasped his shaft. Slowly, she began to stroke it, and she felt the muscle stiffening with each movement. Her head dipped forward, and she shut her eyes. Damen nuzzled his cheek against hers. Together, they used their hands to bring each other to aching need, and then Damen rolled her to her back.

He grabbed a condom from his pants pocket and worked it into place. Then he spread her legs and nestled between them. Her heart pounded, and she found she was a little nervous. When her fingernails dug into his arms, he stilled. She didn't want him to stop, but he moved off her.

"Damen."

"Come here. Climb on top of me."

She gazed at him. "Really?"

"Really. Sit up. You're in control, okay?"

Funny how he told her she was in control, but he was telling her what to do. She did climb atop him though and straddled his hips. Damen massaged her thighs, and she took her time sinking down toward his cock. Her folds parted, and the thick head eased inside her. Heaven's jaw went slack, and then she gritted her teeth. She squeezed her eyes shut until she was full of him.

They stayed still a few moments, and she knew by Damen's pants he worked to keep calm. He waited for her to start moving, and she did, rocking on his dick. Sex with Damen was better than every other man she had ever met. If it was his attitude alone, it would be enough, but his big rod drove her insane. The way he used it, pushing her up and letting her down. Over and over, they moved together, pumping and grinding. Heaven felt her pussy getting wetter. She cried out his name, and came hard and with such intensity she collapsed on his chest.

Damen held her in his arms, moving in and out of her pussy. After a long while, he tensed and whispered her name before he found his release. Heaven lay on his chest until he insisted he prove himself again and again.

CHAPTER SEVEN

"He's a slippery one. I'll give you that."

Heaven moved up behind Stefan and Damen with the drinks they had each asked for and handed one to each. "Who's a slippery one?"

Stefan smiled his thanks. "Someone Damen had his bodyguard following. He keeps losing him."

"Shut up, Stefan," Damen ordered.

Stefan scoffed. "You sound like Creed."

Heaven tensed, and Damen touched her cheek in a fleeting caress. "Not what you think. Forget about it."

"Are you sure?" She looked from one man to the other, but since Damen had warned his brother to be quiet, neither seemed ready to tell her what they were talking about. Well, it didn't matter anyway. She didn't want to hear what his bodyguard was doing. Since that first time, she hadn't seen more than a glimpse of him. The man was big, but he must seriously be part ninja or something. Good riddance.

"Thanks for the drink," Damen said. He turned to Stefan. "Now, about your brother."

"*My* brother?" Stefan laughed.

"He's yours when he's being an asshole."

"Watch your mouth, Damen. You're in front of a lady."

Damen swallowed his drink in a couple gulps. "She is a lady, but Heaven knows how my mouth works."

She dropped the damn tray on the floor. Damen knew good and well what he insinuated when he said it like that, and probably everybody else did too. Not that he made a secret of wanting her now that they were lovers. They hadn't admitted to anything, but he seemed more apt to show it off, especially in front of Tiff. Then Heaven had to deal with that jealous heifer's attitude.

Heaven stomped away from Damen before he could say something else, glad they were at least closed to the public right now. She entered the kitchen on the tail end of Tiff's complaint to the *plongeur*. "This place is the most unprofessional restaurant I have ever worked in."

Rene, the executive chef, spun away from the stove, a rarity to the point that Heaven sometimes wondered if she could pick him out of a lineup. Maybe if the group had their backs turned, she could finger him.

"Then, *chère,*" Rene growled, "perhaps this is not the place for you!"

"Ohhh," the *plongeur* sing-songed, "don't insult Rene's kingdom. He might slice you down, chick."

Tiff scowled at them and then tossed a look of pure dislike at Heaven. She flounced past on her way out of the kitchen.

"Maybe she'll move on to Stefan now that Damen's taken," someone said.

"Or back to Creed because who knows what's going on with Shada and him," another added.

Heaven paid them little mind and walked back to the employee's change room. Her shift had ended, and before the next started, she needed to get out of there. Maybe she would visit Gideon's class tonight to see where he was in his self-defense training and whether it looked like he was enjoying himself. She didn't like the idea of it, but if he wanted to be strong and able to take care of himself, she didn't want to stand in the way because of her own fears.

After slipping out of the restaurant while her lover was preoccupied with something else, she headed toward the community center rather than home. She smiled, thinking of her little scrawny boy. So many times, she had assured him he would grow bigger with time. She believed it based on his dad and his uncles. They were all three tall, strapping men. Her dad wasn't anything to sneeze at either, even though her mother had been average for a woman. Either way, Heaven loved her baby boy. If he were a midget, she'd adore him. She laughed at that thought and shook her head.

I should probably tell him I'm coming in case he gets embarrassed. She dug into her purse for her phone but couldn't find it. Her pockets were empty too, and she cursed. The phone was in her apron at work. She'd meant to take it out. Now she had to go back. Well, whatever. She had only walked a couple blocks.

Heaven doubled back to Marquette's and walked inside. Almost the entire crowd of employees stood in the dining room. She wondered if there was another meeting taking place and no one had bothered telling her about it.

"What's up?" she said and moved closer to the group. The dish washer looked back at her, and her eyes widened in fear and shock. Heaven frowned. What the heck was that about?

Curiosity got the best of her, so she pushed through toward the front, and then she spotted all three brothers standing shoulder to shoulder, facing someone else—someone squat but with muscles that could bring down an elephant. At least she had always thought so, and Leon worked as a bouncer in a New York nightclub. Heaven's eyes burned. Her heart constricted in disbelief. Why was he here, not just in New Orleans, but in Marquette's?

"Look," Leon said, before Heaven could speak, "all I want to know is where Heaven and my son are. I already stopped by her apartment, but she and Gideon weren't there."

"Gideon?" Damen said. Heaven felt her world falling apart.

Leon sneered at Damen. "Yeah, Gideon Burk. He's my son. I thought I convinced Heaven not to come down here with some lame ass story that Gideon is your boy just to get some money, but then I found out she came down here anyway."

An eruption of gasps rose from everyone gathered around. Heaven found her voice and she burst through the crowd to stand before Damen. "That's a lie!"

He stared at her in silence.

Creed's eyes aimed at her were two chips of emerald ice. "Which part, Heaven?"

She shook so badly, she couldn't form words, and she knew it made her look guilty. Leon was a bastard. He knew they had no such conversation about her coming to New Orleans to ask for money for Gideon.

"I told him who Gideon's dad was," she mumbled, and regretted it every day since.

"Yeah, years go," Leon said.

"Last year." She hadn't had the guts to tell him she was leaving then, but that was when she knew she would. Somehow something inside her had grown strong enough to resist Leon. Twelve tormented months followed until she had made the move. That was after so much time under Leon's cruel fists.

"Oh, last year?" Creed gave a sharp, angry laugh. "It took you twelve months to come up with your plan, or was it to perfect it, to line up everyone you needed for references, get in here, work with my brother, have an affair with him."

"An affair!" Leon rounded on her, his face an angry mask. All she saw was him coming at her, punishing her again like he always did in her room where nobody was there to help her.

She stumbled backward, and the tears she had kept control of sprang from her eyes and fell down her cheeks. Swiping at them, she bypassed the crowd while still putting distance between her and Leon.

"Heaven," Damen said, but she couldn't figure out from his tone or his expression if he hated her and believed the lies Leon told like his brother did.

"Leave her, Damen," Creed ordered. "Heaven, get whatever you have in the back, and take it with you. You're fired."

Humiliated, she ran around everybody to head toward the back. Her throat had closed, and she couldn't even stand up for herself. The more she thought of that fact, the wilder her emotions ran, making it harder to put together two words.

"Wait a minute, Heaven," Leon snapped. "You're not going anywhere. I want to know where my boy is."

Leon was putting on a real show. Not only had he never

cared one bit about Gideon, she and Leon hadn't been together long enough for him to think Gideon was his. He knew it, but he wanted to crush her dream of having her baby know his daddy. She hated Leon and wished she had never met him.

She had almost reached the kitchen door when he grabbed her arm and jerked her around. Heaven screamed.

"Get your hands off her," Damen barked. She had never heard such a tone from him. He charged toward them, as the same time, calling, "Guy!"

The next instant, Leon's punishing grip was gone, and he was on the floor huffing and curled in the fetal position, clutching his stomach. Heaven looked up from huge, meaty Leon to bigger Guy hovering over him.

"Ms. Heaven, are you okay?" Guy asked.

She'd never heard his voice, but it matched his size. Shrinking away in full on panic mode, she just stared at him. Damen appeared in front of her and wrapped his arms around her. He dipped his head and touched his lips to her cheek. "It's okay. Everything is going to be fine. Shh, Heaven. You're safe."

Why was he still being nice? Didn't he believe Leon? She didn't know what to think or do, and she was so damn embarrassed. Of course, that wasn't enough, because she clutched his shirtsleeves and promptly hurled all over him.

"I'm fine, Damen," Heaven said, balling tissue in her hand and standing on the street outside Marquette's. She had already cleaned herself up, and apparently he and his brothers kept a change of clothes and had access to a shower. Heaven had refused to use it, wanting to get home, so she had made use of the staff bathroom and changed into her work clothes. After all, most of the damage had been done to Damen. "I need to get going so I can…"

"Pick up Gideon?" he asked, raising his eyebrows.

She turned away from him, hating that she still felt shaky but hoping it didn't show. Leon wasn't in the restaurant when she came out of the bathroom, and she didn't know where he was. "Leon said he stopped by my place before coming here. I didn't give him my address, but if he did find out where I live, I don't want him there."

Damen started in alarm. "Is Gideon there?"

"No, he's at the rec center this afternoon."

"Then I'll escort you," he insisted.

"I don't—"

Damen blocked her path when she moved forward. "Is Leon the man who hurt you, Heaven?"

She didn't answer.

"I know I said I wouldn't bring it up again, but when I said that I thought our pasts were our pasts. This situation shows me I was wrong."

Her energy didn't allow her to argue with him. He was probably saying his thoughts about her were wrong. The positive direction she had found coming here faded into darkness.

"Answer me, Heaven." He spoke gently.

"Yes, Leon used to hit me. There, you happy? I admitted it." To her disgust, tears fell from her eyes again. She scrubbed them away hard and angry. Damen pulled her hand down and held onto it. She tugged, but he wouldn't let go, and when a car drew up to the curb, he opened the back door and insisted she get in.

"Give Guy the address," Damen said.

She hesitated, but it looked like they weren't going anywhere until she did. Heaven mumbled it, and the bodyguard nodded. Damen kept her plastered to his side with an arm around her shoulders. She turned her head and stared out the opposite window.

Before they could pull off, Creed appeared on the sidewalk and tapped on the window. Damen pressed the button to lower the window. Heaven refused to look at Creed, but she felt his animosity. "Are you seriously going to believe this woman, Damen?"

"Talk to you later, bro."

"Damen! It's not like we haven't had to field bullshit like this before."

Heaven grew cold. She hugged herself and dipped her head lower. The whir of the window motor sounded, and from the corner of her eye, she saw Damen give Guy the signal to leave. Guy turned right onto Bourbon Street, heading back in the direction of her home.

"Tell me something, Heaven," Damen said.

She waited for him to go on.

"Did you know Gideon came to the restaurant?"

She gasped and looked at him. "What? That's not possible."

"He did. I'm assuming you never told him about me."

Guilt assailed her. "I did but not your name."

"Well, I suspect he found out on his own. He's been coming by regularly. We didn't know who he was, but we all made friends with him. He's a really good kid."

"T-thank you. Um, I need to clean up at home, and then I can handle things after that, and—"

Damen's expression and tone when he spoke held a dead calm that made her nervous. "You've insinuated Gideon is my son, and you expect me to drop you off and go about my merry way? He's visited me, I think, in the hope that I'm his dad. What do you expect to do now, Heaven? Run away again?"

They pulled up at her apartment. Damen stepped out of the car and helped her out. He leaned down to the window Guy lowered. "Wait out here, and stay on the alert. I don't know if that man was all talk or not."

"Yes, sir."

Damen held out a hand as if to guide her to the building. She had no choice but to go along with what he wanted. At the steps, she glanced up and down the street, but there was no sign of Leon.

Heaven unlocked the door to her second floor apartment and let Damen in. While she hadn't replaced everything she had left behind in New York, she thought she'd done a decent enough job so Damen could see they weren't living in squalor. She wasn't rich, and she had to work to pay her bills, but she didn't need his money.

"I'm going to take a shower and change clothes," she said. "Make yourself comfortable."

He nodded in silence, and she went off to her bedroom. After shutting the bedroom door and locking it, something she wasn't used to, she stripped and stepped into a hot shower. Her heart hurt, her pride was bruised, and depression hung heavy. Damen had said at the start of their second affair she could disappear if she wanted to. Something told her, for him, Gideon changed things. The question was, in what way?

When Heaven was dressed, she walked out to the living room and didn't find Damen. She thought he had left until she heard a sound in Gideon's room. Damen stood in the middle of the disaster area that was her son's room, unpacked but clothes and other junk everywhere. The only items with any kind of order were his CDs. No one except Gideon ever bought them, and he had a vast collection, not to mention all the songs she knew were on the laptop she had bought him.

Damen stooped and ran a finger along one stack of CDs. "He's got some interesting music here. I can't believe he's so young and likes some of this stuff."

"From birth, Gideon seemed obsessed with sound."

Damen glanced at her, and a pang of guilt hit her again. He turned away. "I've been teaching him a little on the guitar."

She gasped. "You're kidding? He never wanted to play an instrument. My dad thought I should force him, said it would give him some discipline, but I wanted Gideon to go wherever his heart leads him."

"The heart doesn't always know the best course."

She put her hands on her hips. "Are you trying to say my dad was right?"

"No, I wouldn't force Gideon to do what he hated either."

"Well I need to go. He'll be wondering where I am."

"*We* need to go."

"Damen, you're being stubborn about this. I think we both need time to think…"

"You've had eleven years."

"If you're mad at me, say so."

"Isn't it obvious? Of course I'm pissed, Heaven. You didn't give me the chance to know my son."

She spun on her heel and marched out of the room. He followed. Heaven grabbed her purse and keys and started for the door. "Well, you don't have to worry about me disappearing. I'm not going to run away. The whole reason I came here was so Gideon could get to know you, not to get your money!"

"I didn't believe that."

She stopped and turned back to him. "Wait, what?"

He stepped closer. Her nerve endings jangled with electricity off of him, but he didn't touch her. "You made the wrong choice not to tell me about Gideon, but I don't believe you're after my money."

Damen might not think she had ulterior motives, but anger continued to punctuate his words. He hadn't admitted what he would do about Gideon from here on out. Maybe he was still trying to figure that part out.

They left the apartment and climbed into the waiting car. When they arrived at the rec center, once again, Damen insisted on joining her. The woman behind the reception desk walked them through the procedure for visitor's passes even though she recognized Heaven. The diligence eased Heaven's mind a little when she thought of Leon showing up.

As soon as Heaven and Damen strode into the room where Gideon was having his martial arts lesson, she knew Damen had been speaking the truth about Gideon visiting. Her son's eyes widened, and he ran straight for them, ignoring the command from his instructor.

"You're here together," Gideon shouted for the whole world to hear. Then Gideon focused on her. She'd never seen a look of such desperation in her son's expression. "Mom, does he know?"

She hesitated. Damen hadn't said a word. He stared at Gideon just as stunned. She wished they'd both snap out of it.

"Maaaa!"

"Yes, Gideon. Shut that noise up." She mouthed sorry to the instructor.

Gideon grabbed Damen's hand. "Dad, come and look at

what I can do. Check it out."

If anything, Damen's gaze lost even more focus when Gideon called him dad. He followed Gideon across the room and stood near him while Gideon went through a series of moves his instructor called out to the class. Heaven watched the two of them, father and son, and she found herself getting choked up again. She ached to know what Damen thought at that moment.

Then she saw it, Damen glowing with pride and nodding. He called encouragement to Gideon, and her scrawny little pipsqueak stood a few inches bigger. Damen hated violence. She knew that from talking to him years ago, when he confessed to her how Creed had been punched so many times by their dad. His older brother took the pain so Damen and Stefan wouldn't have to.

In spite of Damen's personal feelings in that arena, he seemed to support Gideon in his choice. Yet, she knew from Gideon's lecturing her after each class martial arts wasn't about fighting.

Class ended, and Damen and Heaven followed the chatterbox to the car. Heaven shook her head. "He's not usually this talkative."

Damen smiled. "I know."

She looked at him. They climbed into the car, and Gideon bounced forward in the seat. "Hey, Guy."

"Hey, little buddy."

Heaven blinked in surprise when the bodyguard and her son gave each other high fives.

"Can't catch me," Gideon joked.

The bodyguard smirked. "I *thought* you were escaping me on purpose."

"Yup," Gideon laughed. "I saw you at my dad's restaurant,

but at first I didn't know you were his bodyguard. I couldn't let anyone get near my mom. Then I kept doing it because it was fun."

"Scamp," the big man grumbled, but his gaze held amusement. Heaven's fear of him eased a little.

Damen hugged Gideon. "Good job taking care of your mom."

Gideon looked at him seriously. "That was my job until you came. Dad, are you going to take care of her now? She needs you."

"Gideon! Boy, shut your mouth." She frowned at him, but neither he nor Damen seemed to pay her any mind. Father and son looked back and forth at each other, unwavering.

Damen nodded. "That's exactly what I'm going to do, son."

CHAPTER EIGHT

Heaven sat across from Damen, stirring the food about on her plate. Eating was the last thing on her mind right now, but that didn't appear to be the case with Damen and Gideon. Her son shoved food between his lips only a fraction slower than Damen. She rolled her eyes at the two of them.

Gideon leaned toward his dad, and Damen met him halfway. "This food is good but not like Marquette's."

Damen agreed.

"I know you didn't beg for food like I don't feed you, Gideon?" She glared at him.

"I had my allowance."

"You don't get that much allowance."

He ducked his head.

"If I give him dinner, how is that different from you giving it to him?" Damen said.

Heaven snapped her teeth together. Gideon looked from her to his dad and back again. "Are you fighting?"

"No, of course not." Heaven knew how much it upset Gideon to hear arguing. She looked at Damen and willed him in silence to back her up. He was mad, but he could hide it for now. *Please,* she begged with her eyes.

"We're not fighting, Gideon." Damen squeezed his shoulder. "How about that spinach? Good, huh?"

Gideon eyed his dad as if he had lost his mind. Heaven laughed. "You're not fooling him with that one."

"What if I reminded him about Popeye?"

Gideon took a long sip of his soda. "Who's Popeye?"

"Never mind."

Heaven shook her head. "There are ways I get him to eat veggies. Sometimes it's hit and miss. Some offhand comment like 'good, huh' will never get it done."

Damen took his defeat with humor. "Okay, something to learn. I'm surprised you didn't threaten him with 'you can't leave the table until those veggies are gone.'"

"Oh, just because I'm black, I'm a tyrant?"

Damen's eyes widened. "No, I didn't mean—"

Both Heaven and Gideon cracked up at that one, and Gideon ribbed his dad. "She was just kidding. Don't fall for it."

"How did you know? She sounded serious." Damen looked confused.

"Because Mom has a friend in New York who uses that on her all the time."

"On your mom? But…"

Heaven grinned and waved her hand. "It's just a stupid inside joke, Damen. Don't worry about it. Basically, she claims I say something or do something because she's black. Yeah, I know. We're both black, but it's funny because of that. Don't you see? It's… forget it. If I have to explain, it's not funny anymore."

The man looked confused but she had broken the ice between them. He loosened up more, and a lot of her tension ebbed away. They chatted almost like old friends.

"Mom, do you know about my sister?" Gideon asked out of the blue.

And there goes the peace.

"Yes, Gideon. Anita. She's your half-sister."

"She's his sister," Damen corrected. "We don't need to add halves and wholes to it."

"That's a good policy." She wanted so bad to blurt out if that meant he fully accepted Gideon, but she didn't want to have the conversation in front of Gideon.

"You haven't seen her much at Marquette's since you've been there, Heaven."

She waved her hands and widened her eyes. Damen fell silent.

"When were you at Marquette's, Mom?"

She pursed her lips. "When I had business there and you didn't."

That shut him up because he knew better than to sneak off without telling her. He could have gotten hurt or snatched, and she would never have known. Just thinking about it scared the hell out of her, and it must have shown on her face because Damen reached across the table to take her hand.

"It's fine now. Gideon won't be sneaking off anymore, will you?"

Her son's face fell, and he looked at Damen. "I can come by the restaurant as much as I want, can't I, Dad?"

Heaven wondered how many times the boy needed to say dad in one evening. She didn't blame him, and the spark of jealousy knowing she would share her baby from now on was just that—a spark.

"You can come with your mom's permission, and with an escort," Damen said.

"An escort? You mean somebody taking me like a little baby?" Gideon couldn't sound more outraged. "It's only ten blocks, and if I come right after school, it's still daylight out."

Damen stroked his hair. "Do you know who I am, Gideon?"

"Damen Marquette."

Damen laughed. "Yes, but I mean other than my name."

"You own a restaurant with good food with my uncles." Gideon's eyes glittered.

"Yes, I do, but there're other facts about your dad you don't know. I'm not going to go into detail right now, but it will soon be public knowledge that you're my son. Unfortunately, that changes the equation a little."

"What equation?"

Even if Gideon didn't understand, Heaven got it right away, and she rubbed a hand over her eyes. She hadn't thought that far. Damen and his brothers had to be protected at all times being billionaires. Greedy, evil people got stupid ideas and could try something. Now she realized Nita must also have someone watching her when she wasn't with her dad. As Damen said, Gideon would need an escort whether she or he liked it or not. Some of those evil people with ideas might try to get to Damen through her son. She couldn't live with that.

Heaven became aware Damen still held her hand when he squeezed it. She looked at him, and he met her gaze with a serious and determined one of his own. "I won't let anyone hurt either of you ever again."

"Damen, you can't make that promise." She looked away and withdrew her hand from his.

After Damen settled the check, and she didn't argue because Gideon was there, they left the restaurant together. Gideon talked Guy's ear off behind them, and Damen took her arm ahead of the bodyguard and their son.

Did I really just think of him as our son?

"Heaven."

She glanced over at Damen.

"I want you and Gideon to move in with me and Nita."

She gaped. "Ah, what now?"

"If you feel more conformable, we can get married."

"Are you out of your mind, Damen? Marry you? And can you toss it out there with any less emotion?"

He smiled. "I'll be happy to get down on one knee."

"Your joke isn't funny."

"I'm dead serious."

"That's not possible."

"Not possible it wasn't a joke or that you can marry me?"

"Both."

"Why?"

"Because you don't love me."

He stopped walking and pulled her to a stop. On cue, Guy called Gideon's attention to a storefront that looked like a voodoo shop. Damen noticed and called over to them, "No scary stories, Guy."

"Yes, sir."

When Damen turned back to her, he caught her studying his face, and he grinned. "I had to sleep with Nita a few times when she was younger because *I* was afraid of the dark. Or so she told me."

Heaven smiled despite her confusion. She'd been there

with Gideon too. Now, he wouldn't be caught dead running to her if he was afraid. They grew up too fast. Never mind that. She focused on the subject at hand.

"Why would you ask me to move in or marry you?"

"We don't have to love each other, Heaven," he explained in that matter-of-fact way that was pissing her off. "We get along great."

"We were lovers. That doesn't constitute 'getting along great.'"

"Are lovers, and it's a strong start."

"Says a man, and I'm not sure we should continue as lovers. It might send the wrong message to Gideon—and Nita for that matter."

"It sends the exact message I want, that we're a family."

"Damen."

"Think about it, Heaven."

"You haven't even thought about it. You just found out about Gideon today, and while I know he's yours, you don't know. I mean why aren't you demanding a paternity test or something? You're freaking rich. I could be after your billions."

"The very fact that you're suggesting such a thing says you aren't. I'm not a fool. I know it's possible. You heard what my brother said. We get letters that go straight to lawyers."

"You have other kids?"

"No."

She must have looked doubtful.

"I'm positive, and you and I, that was the only time I wasn't careful. Nita came along after I was married."

"Well your brothers wouldn't like it, especially Creed."

"Let me handle my brothers."

"Damen, I want to be in love."

"Aren't you?"

She stared at him. "W-what?"

He skimmed a thumb over her cheek. "Aren't you in love?"

She turned away. "You've got a seriously big head, you know that?"

Damen stood close behind her, and she wanted to run in the opposite direction before she got hurt again. Life had taught her to be strong, but in the face of this man, life was pushing its damn luck.

"You love me, Heaven." He covered her lips when she would have protested. "It's not my ego that makes me say it but deduction."

She rolled her eyes.

"You said I don't love you, which told me you already knew your feelings. In this kind of situation, a woman would be more concerned about her emotions in a relationship."

"Don't presume to tell me what I think and feel, as a woman or otherwise."

"You're saying I'm wrong?"

"Yes!" She lied because it was the only way to save face. Heaven didn't need his pity or the bone he thought he was throwing her by proposing marriage. "I don't need your money, your name, or yo—"

"Heaven, I didn't mean to offend you."

She ignored him and started walking again. He nodded to the bodyguard, and the four of them moved toward her home.

"Heaven."

"Stop, Damen. I'm not doing it."

"You want love," he went on stubbornly. "Isn't it possible for me to love you? I mean love you the way you want me to.

I care about you already as my lover and as my son's mother."

"You sure were quick to accept us. I don't trust it."

"What if I told you I'm being selfish?"

She squinted at him.

"I've never wanted to be a single dad."

Her mouth fell open.

"Family is important to me, as it is with both my brothers. Our parents weren't there as they should have been, and I see the effects my brothers and I have had to overcome regarding it. I want greater stability for Nita and Gideon."

Heaven stared at him. His words blew her mind, and she fumbled for a response. "There's no guarantee our home would be a happy one, Damen. You have to look at this realistically. What if two months after we're married you fall in love with someone else? O-or I do?" she forced herself to add.

"I won't."

"You might."

"Listen." He stopped walking again, halting the entire group. "I'm asking you to take a chance. It's not a bad gamble, is it? To be with me and to have Gideon with his dad full time? I'm an easygoing kind of guy, and I wouldn't spend time trying to force you to be something you're not. Finally, I've been married before. I don't mind risking a second failure."

She wrinkled her nose. "Is this a business proposition or a marriage proposal?"

His gaze twinkled. "If it's business don't misunderstand. I'm expecting sexual benefits."

"Hm, what a surprise."

He linked his fingers with hers, and they walked that way until they reached her apartment. Even that much, she knew gave Gideon ideas, but she didn't have the will to pull away.

They walked inside, and Gideon spent time with his dad, showing him his music and other favorites in his room. Guy disappeared somewhere outside, and Heaven dropped onto the couch.

Heaven must have fallen asleep because the next time she opened her eyes, Damen sat beside her with her feet drawn onto his lap. "What are you doing?"

He smiled. "Watching you sleep."

"You're weird." She stood up and walked into the bedroom to check on Gideon. Her cell said it was pretty late, and her son stretched across the bed fully dressed. Heaven wiggled his shoulder. "Gideon, get up and get ready for bed."

"But it's the weekend," he whined. "No school tomorrow, so I can stay up late with dad."

"Yeah, well you're not up. You're sleeping."

Gideon tried sitting up but yawned and lay still.

"Let me handle it."

Heaven looked around to find Damen coming into the room. She stepped aside and watched as he made short work of Gideon's clothes. Then he glanced at her. "Pajamas?"

"Boxers and a tee is all he'll keep on."

He nodded, and Heaven handed over the clean T-shirt. Damen worked as if he had prepared a child for bed many times. She supposed he did with Nita, and she recalled what he said about not wanting to be a single dad.

When Damen was done, he straightened and frowned down at Gideon. "Should I get him up to go to the bathroom?"

"Don't worry. He'll go if he needs to."

"Nita wet the bed until she was six, but don't tell her I told you."

Heaven heard sadness in his voice even if he tried to keep the words light. She squeezed his arm. "The separation from her mom maybe."

He shrugged. "Come on. Let's go out to the living room."

They clicked off Gideon's light, and sat on the couch together. Heaven was just about to ask him where Nita was tonight when someone knocked on the front door. "Who the heck?" she wondered.

Damen patted her thigh. "Stay there. I'll get it, probably Guy."

Heaven stiffened. She didn't want the bodyguard hanging out in her apartment. When Damen opened the door, she found it was Guy, but he was holding Nita, who was sound asleep.

"Thanks. I've got her." Damen took his daughter into his arms, and Guy nodded and turned away. Damen looked at her. "Does that couch pull out?"

"Are you serious? Damen, it's late, and you bring her here?"

"There's no school tomorrow."

"You sound like Gideon. Hang on. Let me get some sheets. Jeez, I feel like you're trying to railroad me."

"Never. I'm just demonstrating the full package." He grinned. She glared at him.

Heaven's couch was a pullout bed. She didn't expect anyone to visit, but for some reason, she always liked to be prepared just in case. After she had made up the bed, Damen tucked his daughter in, who was already dressed in pink pajamas.

"Who had her?" she wondered.

"Her nanny."

"She has a full time nanny?" Heaven's eyes widened.

"No, not full." He brushed his daughter's hair from her forehead and kissed it. Then he straightened. "I only allow her to take care of Nita when I can't. Otherwise, I do everything for her."

"Do you have servants?"

He looked guilty, and she put her hands on her hips, pursing her lips.

"Someone cleans the house, but I do laundry."

"You do laundry?" She didn't mean to raise her voice with the shock.

"Shh." He reached for her hand and pulled her to him. They shut off the lights and headed into her bedroom. "Yes. She's eight. At the beginning, I wasn't alone, and I wasn't rich. Afterward, I wanted to hold onto caring for her, to keep us close as long as possible. I think I might have gone too far in the opposite direction."

"What does that mean?"

"Nita is a little spoiled."

"I heard a few stories at Marquette's."

He looked offended.

"Don't worry. It's nothing that can't be reversed when you stop letting your daughter push you around."

"I don't let—oh, who am I kidding." He rubbed the back of his head. "I was trying to make up for her mother abandoning her. By your expression, you heard about that too."

They lay across the bed together, and Damen drew her into his arms. Heaven told herself she let him because he probably needed it discussing such a painful subject. Had nothing to do with her desires.

You're lying in your own head.

"Vida was smart and beautiful, and she had come here to attend school from Mexico. She lured me in with the lilt in her accent, and when I pissed her off, she lapsed into her language to curse me. I pissed her off on purpose sometimes and pretended not to know what she was saying."

Heaven looked at him. "You speak Spanish?"

He shrugged. "I was bored once."

"How many other times were you bored?"

He cleared his throat.

"Damen?"

"Four, but it's not as impressive as it sounds."

"I'm not sure how. You speak four languages?"

"Five if you include English."

She smacked his arm. "I could never keep up with you."

"I'm not looking for someone to keep up with me, Heaven. I know I'm as you say weird."

"I didn't mean that."

"Yes, you did, but it's okay. I am what I am."

"You're funny, too."

"Don't forget sexy."

"And big-headed."

He chuckled and then grew serious. "I want you to understand."

She nodded. They both sat up and leaned against the headboard. Heaven put space between them because she wasn't sure she could handle more with him talking about Vida. She didn't know the woman and disliked her, an immature feeling that had only a part to do with that poor little girl.

"Vida was young, and she fell in love with me, and she was so full of life. The only way I can describe it is like a butterfly flitting about from experience to experience. We were just getting our business to take off, so I was busy a lot. I couldn't always be there, and that was a problem. She thought she would get me to focus on her by getting pregnant. It worked for a while because knowing my daughter was coming was the most amazing gift."

Heaven stiffened, wondering if he would recall she hadn't let him experience the anticipation of Gideon. For a while he said nothing, and she knew he was thinking about it.

"You can tell me every detail about before and after?" he said, and she saw the hope in his gaze. "Do you have pictures?"

She smiled. "Yeah, I'll show you tomorrow."

He nodded.

"So what happened with Vida?"

He sighed and tilted his head back against the headboard. Heaven watched as his Adam's apple bobbed up and down. Her fingers were drawn to stroke his neck, but she resisted. Damen looked at her, and she lost another battle to pull his glasses off. He allowed it but then claimed a reward by kissing her lips.

"Nita was two when she met someone else and decided to leave. Truth is over that two years, it was hell. She hated the responsibility of raising a child, saying she couldn't be free to do what she wanted."

"I'm so sorry. You two deserved better than that." Heaven kissed him again. "I'd kill if someone tried to tell me I couldn't take care of Gideon. He's my world."

"I'm jealous."

She blinked at him. "What?"

"I want him to love me like he loves you. It's childish."

She laughed. "Uh, did you hear the number of times that boy called you dad? At least a million."

He grinned and flattened a hand over his heart. "And it shot me right here every time. I can't believe how great tonight was. *I* would kill for more of that, Heaven."

"I get it."

"Do you? I know it seems sudden to you."

"Not for Gideon. Truth is, from the beginning I told him all about you, some of the funny things you used to say, the way you acted, how awkward you were when we met. I've been telling Gideon about you for years, so when you wish he'd love you like he loves me, trust and believe, he does already."

Damen stared at her in awe. "You did that?"

"Yeah, I did that."

He held up a finger. "More evidence that you love me."

"Shut up!" She turned away, kicking herself, but Damen drew her back to him. His arms were a vice, gentle but firm in not allowing her to escape. With talk of all she had shared with Gideon about Damen over the years, she suddenly remembered the hoodie. The gray beat up one Gideon loved to wear was the one Damen had leant her all those years ago when they got caught in the rain. Oh yeah, that boy loved his daddy all right. No doubt about it.

One of Damen's hands splayed over her belly and slid toward her pussy. "So, what do you think about getting frisky tonight?"

She smacked his hand and dragged it away from her goodies. "No way. We've got two kids in the house."

"We'll have two kids when we're married."

"I didn't tell you I'll marry you."

"Well, even if you don't, which I'm hoping you will, we'll still have the kids. Come on, beautiful, let's make love."

"Go sleep on the couch with your daughter."

"But…"

She climbed off the bed and headed to the bathroom. "I'm taking a shower, and I'm going to crash. Good night."

As she shut the door, she grinned hearing his grumbles of protest.

CHAPTER NINE

Damen opened his eyes to bright sunlight and noise. He started to ask Nita to watch cartoons downstairs, but then he recalled they weren't at their house. They were in Heaven's apartment, and he lay on the pullout bed in the living room, not the most comfortable mattress. All he recalled of the night was Nita's knees in his back and a hand slung against his head. For an eight-year-old, she slept like a wild animal. He would have preferred to spoon Heaven's snuggable ass.

While Damen had visions of what else he'd like to do with Heaven, Nita's high-pitched tones cut across his dreams. "Why are we at your house?"

No answer. Damen knew she spoke to Gideon.

"Hey, are you listening to me?" Nita's voice rose.

"Get off," Gideon snapped. "You're noisy!"

"If you answer me, I won't have to pull them out. Why do you listen to music so much? You're like Uncle Stefan. It's creepy."

"You're creepy!"

"Shut up."

Damen shoved the covers off his head. "Kids, stop arguing."

"She started it."

"He started it."

Damen groaned.

Heaven appeared. "Both of you cool it, now."

"Yes, ma'am," Gideon said right away.

No answer from Nita.

"Nita?" Damen sat up.

She looked at him with wide innocent eyes. "Yes, Daddy?"

"Did you hear Heaven?"

"Yes."

"Then answer."

She gave a dramatic sigh.

Not for the first time, Damen felt embarrassed at her behavior. His face warmed. "Nita."

"Fine. I heard you," she said to Heaven.

He was about to give Heaven an apology, but she marched past the couch to the narrow space in front of the TV. Both kids sat too close. Heaven bent over and fingered Nita's chin higher. "Little girl, when I tell you to do something, you say 'yes, ma'am.' You're not going to disrespect me in my own house. You can pull that with your daddy but not me. Got it?"

Nita looked around. "This is an apartment, not a house."

"Excuse me?" Heaven's voice had gone deeper and harsher than he had ever heard it.

"Yes, ma'am."

Damen stared at the woman in awe. He had never won an argument with Nita because he could never use simple logic

106

with her, or for that matter command her to do something and she just do it. His mocha beauty had earned greater respect from him than she already had.

"Okay, everybody up," Heaven announced.

Damen's moans blended with the kids', but he figured he would make an example of himself to Nita if nothing else. As Heaven fired off orders for him to fold the sheets he and Nita had used and tuck in the sofabed, Gideon and Nita were to go brush their teeth, shower, and get dressed.

"It's Saturday," Nita whined.

Heaven stood with her hands on her hips. "Yes, and it's ten thirty. You slept in. Now, I want a clear living room and dining room while I get some breakfast on the table. After you're cleaned up, you can go back to your shows."

Nita spun to Damen. "Why is your waitress telling *me* what to do, Daddy? And why did we sleep here?"

"Crap, forgot about that," Heaven said.

Damen looked at Gideon. So he didn't tell. He was proud of the kid, or maybe Gideon didn't want to admit the relationship. Damen thought back to yesterday and the moment he realized Gideon was his. Shock, disbelief, and oddly enough, hope had gone through him. He had recalled Heaven from the first moment she walked into Marquette's. How could he forget? She'd been so beautiful, and when she disappeared, he hadn't understood why. Then later, she stood in his restaurant admitting Gideon was his.

Damen considered it, and he knew he wouldn't have believed the story if he hadn't met and gotten to know Gideon on his own. While everyone had been shouting around him, Damen reviewed every detail of his interaction with his son. He recalled the longing in Gideon's eyes when he looked at Damen and the gentle personality that was similar to Stefan's.

Gideon didn't have a lot of outward appearance that matched the Marquettes, except maybe the nose, but that could be almost any person of European descent.

The fact was, he recalled how Gideon had mannerisms, which matched Damen's mother. That was another of Damen's studies, but in this case it was for a school paper. Research showed children could inherit mannerisms of family members even if they hadn't met those family members in person. Of course, when Damen hung out with Gideon, not knowing who he was, he didn't make the connection, but he recalled with total clarity.

The "evidence" was superficial at best, but Damen believed Gideon was his without a doubt. On top of that, Gideon himself believed it, and Damen counted the boy's feelings on the matter much more important than his own. *Especially after meeting that dick who dared to hurt Heaven. He won't ever do it again.*

"Why don't we all sit down and talk," Damen suggested. "Nita, come here."

His daughter wrinkled her nose at him, but she complied. He drew her down beside him on the couch and kept an arm about her shoulders. Damen crooked a finger at Gideon when he hesitated and patted the seat on his other side. Gideon was beside him like a shot. Heaven took the spot on the other side of Gideon.

Damen cleared his throat. He met Heaven's gaze over Gideon's head, and she nodded. He turned back to Nita. "Sweetheart, a long time ago, I met Heaven in college. That was before you were born and before I met your mom."

"Oh, a really old friend." Nita scoffed and started to rise, but Damen held her in place.

"Hey, I'm not that old, thank you."

Damen chuckled. "She's eight, Heaven. Let it go."

Heaven pursed her lips.

"Nita, from me…uh…knowing Heaven…we both received a gift."

When Nita wiggled around in impatience, he got straight to it.

"Heaven and I had Gideon together. Gideon is your brother. Now, I want you to understand I love you very much. Nothing will ever change that." He hugged his son closer to his side. "And I love Gideon. Nothing will change that either. From now on, Gideon and Heaven will be a permanent part of our lives."

"Wait," Heaven protested.

"My brother," Nita protested. "He doesn't even look like you, Daddy."

"Neither do you," Gideon shot back.

Damen chuckled. "Nita, Daddy got the short end of the stick in the looks department. You and Gideon got your looks from your beautiful mothers."

Heaven appeared to have eaten something sour. She rolled her eyes at him and stood up. "I'm going to cook breakfast. Do you two like pancakes?"

"Pancakes." Nita seemed to fight with a desire to reject Heaven and Gideon, but pancakes happened to be her favorite.

"Mom always cooks pancakes on the weekend," Gideon told them and lowered his voice. "She doesn't do too good with eggs though, so pretend you only want pancakes and bacon or sausage. I love pancakes, so it's okay."

"Pancakes sounds great," Damen announced and winked at Gideon. His son grinned. "I'll help you. You two, get along. We'll talk some more later."

Damen cleaned up and then joined Heaven in the kitchen. She glanced over at him as he walked in. "Don't you think you should give her a minute to tell you what she's thinking about all this?"

"It's pretty obvious what she's thinking. I figured I'd let it sink in for a little while."

"You mean you ran off before she could say anything."

"I didn't run off, Heaven."

She smirked. "Uh-huh."

"And you didn't?" He leaned against the counter and folded his arms over his chest. She was cute in the morning, but he wanted to see her when she hadn't yet combed her hair or cleaned up. Earlier, she appeared all put together, which told him she had risen before ten thirty.

"I'm making breakfast."

Damen moved up behind her. He had an urge to grind against her ass, and his desire had grown from the night before. Just knowing she was in the same house, lying in her bed, had driven him insane. He wanted to make love to her, but she had denied him. Damen leaned in and breathed her scent at the side of her neck. He rested hands on her waist and let her ass brush his thigh.

"Damen," she breathed. "The kids..."

"Will get used to seeing us together."

"You said Gideon and I are now a permanent part of your lives. Don't you think that's jumping the gun?"

Damen took the bowl of batter from her and started mixing while she prepared the skillet. "I plan to have Gideon in my life forever. You're his mom. It stands to reason we have a permanent connection."

"Oh."

He squeezed her ass. "And when you say yes to marrying

me…"

She slapped his arm.

The four of them ate breakfast at Heaven's small dining table that was a challenge for two let alone four people. Damen insisted on rinsing the dishes and stacking them in the dishwasher, although he ground his teeth while doing it.

Heaven laughed at him. "If you hate it, why don't you move and let me do it?"

"Because you cooked for me. I don't want to be selfish."

"You still owe me, pal. Stacking the dishwasher isn't work."

"Doesn't stop me from hating it."

She laughed. "You're a baby."

Damen smirked. "Waa waa."

Heaven swung away from him laughing, but he caught her and drew her back against him. She struggled to get out of his hold. Damen pressed his lips to her ear and whispered, "Marry me."

"Damen, how long are going to keep asking me?"

"Until you say yes."

"So no isn't an option?"

"Not unless you have a better idea."

She pulled his fingers around that were laced over her belly, and he allowed it. "I do. It's called visitation."

"No!"

She gasped, and he surprised himself at the vehemence in his tone. He hadn't meant to sound so angry or insistent. In fact, he didn't realize he felt so strongly against seeing Gideon only during some kind of schedule.

"I apologize," he said.

Heaven moved away and faced him. "That's what's bothering you, isn't it?"

He couldn't deny it. "Yes."

"Damen, we can't force a relationship just to accommodate the kids. Plenty of them grow up with single parents, and they're fine. It's not ideal, but it can work."

He didn't respond. What she said made sense logically, and he knew there was plenty evidence available to back up that view. None of it changed how he felt. Damen realized in the end, she might not agree to marry him or live with him. He despised the thought while acknowledging it.

"I need to take care of a few things," he said. "I'd like to spend the afternoon and evening with you and Gideon. Are you busy?"

She hesitated and then sighed. "All right. I admit it makes me happy to see Gideon so excited to be with you."

He grinned. "He's not the only one. Besides, you promised me pictures."

"Hold on." She ran out of the kitchen and returned a few moments later with an envelope. "These are for you. I saved them special. I have more, and we can look through them when we meet up again."

Damen's chest tightened, but he took the envelope, paused staring at it a moment, and then peeled open the flap. Inside were two small photographs. Both were of Gideon as an infant. In the first one his son lay sleeping with dark curls slicked to his head, and a white blanket with powder blue stripes covered him. Gideon's skin was much paler than it was now, his hands as white as Damen's before he tanned.

The other photo showed Gideon being held in someone's arms, he assumed Heaven's. This time, Gideon's eyes were open, and he stared into the camera. One arm was raised, tiny fingers curled as if he tried grabbing for the object in front of him but had no motor control to reach it.

Damen raised both photos and the envelope to his forehead, shutting his eyes. He waited for his emotions to calm down, embarrassed for Heaven to see him choked up. "Thank you," he whispered after some time. "This means a lot to me."

She hugged him. "Of course."

"Heaven, can you tell me why you kept him from me?" Damen didn't mean to sound resentful, but he knew he did when she spun away. "I don't blame you."

"Yes, you do, but I understand. If it was the reverse, I'd scratch your eyes out."

He winced.

She looked at him. "I take full responsibility for my choice because it was mine to make."

"But?"

"My dad. Did you know my dad is Alfred Burk?"

"Wait, the English professor? Why didn't I realize that?"

She twisted her hands together. "Because we didn't get along. I almost never saw him, even then. He was supporting me, of course, so when I found out I was pregnant, I told him. He wanted to know who the father was."

"He knew me. He'd become my mentor."

"I know."

Damen couldn't believe the connection, and he had kept up with Professor Burk over the years. The man hadn't mentioned his daughter more than once or twice, and never by name. Could their disagreement be that severe? "You told him about me?"

"Yeah, I told him. He said you deserve to have a better life than to be dragged down by an unplanned pregnancy because I wasn't careful."

Damen's eyes widened. This sounded like fantasy. He

113

knew Professor Burk, or thought he did. As he recalled the many conversations they had had over the years, he realized they centered around learning and whatever scientific advancements interested Damen at the moment, nothing more intimate like a daughter and his own son. The sense of betrayal burned in his veins.

"It took two to make our son," he ground out.

"Yeah, well, my dad didn't see it that way. He saw it as me causing more heartache in your life. He knew about your past."

Damen nodded. "I'd discussed it with him once or twice."

"What about you, Heaven?"

"Huh?"

"What about your past—with him and your mom and…?"

"There's not much to tell." She started to move away again, but he caught her up to his chest. He kissed her lips and felt her tremble a little.

Damen nuzzled her neck. "We'll pick this up later, when you're going to open up to me."

"Damen."

"No arguments." He left her standing in the kitchen to find Gideon. His son sat in his room on the laptop. Nita had sprawled before the television in the living room. Damen wondered if they would ever get along and then recalled the way Heaven handled the two. With time, he decided, working together, they would be a family. "Gideon, what do you say to some sightseeing in New Orleans today?"

Gideon looked up from his computer screen. "Sightseeing?"

"Yeah, we can go anyplace you want to this afternoon."

His son appeared to think about it. "How about a city of

the dead? And there's a new sci-fi movie I want to see."

"You got it, but don't you think you'll be afraid visiting a graveyard?"

"It's different. All the graves are aboveground. I read about it before we moved here."

"Fine. I have to take care of some business, and then it's us four together."

Gideon hesitated. "My…sister doesn't like me."

Damen smiled, liking how Gideon worded it. He'd at least begun to accept Nita. "Give it time. Neither of you have had a sibling before. In fact, this is new to all of us. We're going to make it work though. As a man, can I count on you to help me with your mom and sister?"

Gideon's narrow chest poked out. "Yes, sir."

"Thanks." Now all Damen had to do was bring around a very angry older brother of his own.

Damen paused in Marquette's kitchen. "Someone, a vodka on the rocks, please."

Within moments, he held the glass in his hand, and he knocked back most of the alcohol.

"Isn't it a little early for you?" Shada asked. She kept her back to him as she worked. He heard a sour note in her voice, but he couldn't see her expression. So she and Creed hadn't made up. Great. He had been hoping they did, and it would mean he'd find his brother in a better mood. Not that Creed scared him, but the bear soothed was better than being ripped by his claws—the claws being Creed's temper.

"It's after one," he said.

"Whatever."

Damen waited for more from her, but she said nothing.

He checked her left hand. No ring, but that didn't mean anything either. She'd kept removing it with the excuse that she didn't want it to drop into a pot or get damaged in some other way. No one believed the excuse, least of all Creed. An instance of pity washed over him regarding his brother. His choice wasn't an easy one.

Hell, neither is mine.

Damen finished the drink and set the glass in the sink before heading down the hall. He didn't bother knocking on the door or inquiring of one of the others as to whether Creed was in. Creed was always in if he wasn't in New York. They had hired competent managers for the parent company, and Creed had stepped down as CEO, so New York wasn't as much of an issue.

As soon as Creed spotted him, he frowned. "Ever heard of answering your cell?"

"I had it on silent." Damen shut the door and dropped into his desk chair.

"Damen—"

"Let me get right to it, Creed." Damen pushed his glasses up on his nose. "I've asked Heaven to marry me."

"You fucking *what?*" Creed raged.

"You heard me."

Creed slammed a fist on his desk and surged to his feet, but Damen didn't move from his position. "I suppose she jumped all over it, probably has the gown waiting in the closet."

"She turned me down."

"A ploy."

Damen sighed.

"You can't tell me you believe her. We've had women pretending their bastard children are ours before. This woman was probably fucking several other men at the same time she was with you. Her son—"

Damen clenched his hands atop the desk. "Say what you want about Heaven. I care about her, and I happen to think she's a good woman. I understand you have your doubts about her character because you don't know her. But say one single word against *my* son, and I will forget I hate violence and wipe the floor with your ass."

Creed's eyes grew round in shock. "I wasn't about to. He's just a kid, subject to believe whatever his mother told him. Seeing you so obviously convinced without evidence disgusts me. Damn it, Damen, think. She's after your money. Why can't you see that?"

"Let's say that's true. Gideon *is* mine. Everything I have is his and Nita's. You're saying I should turn my back on him?"

"No, but before you offer her our name, check her out. You saw that guy who came in here yesterday. There might be something to what he's saying. *He* says the boy's his."

"It's always about our name with you, Creed."

His brother ground his teeth.

"You act like the Marquette name is special. It's just another name."

"It's all we had coming up."

"No, *we* are all we had. We are, and we're still here, you, me, and Stefan." A new thought came to Damen. "Other people recognize the name now though. They respect it, and it opens doors. I'm going to adopt Gideon and give him my last name."

"Wait, so he's not your son. You're going to try to take Heaven's son?"

"No, I don't have to take him away from her to adopt him as my responsibility and one of my heirs. I want to be on his birth certificate as his dad, and I want him to carry my last name."

Creed rubbed his eyes. "Damen, I always knew you were stubborn, and you just had to do whatever popped into your head. You, along with Stefan, have pulled some crazy stunts. This—this beats all of it, and it's wrong."

"No, you're wrong. I've made my decision."

"Test him," Creed suggested. "Get a paternity test to make sure. If it turns out he's blood, I will support you in everything you do concerning him."

"Except marrying Heaven?"

"Damen, see reason."

Damen stood up and walked toward the door. "If I get my way, Heaven will be my wife. I hope you'll be at the ceremony and welcome her into the family."

"Hold on."

Damen glanced over his shoulder, tension in his muscles as he expected his brother to continue fighting him on his decision. "What?"

"Why her? You don't love her, right? It could be anyone because you still love Vita. Why get married again at all?"

Damen hesitated to give voice to thoughts that had been swirling in his head since seeing Heaven after so long. He still wasn't clear on everything, but he believed the few words he spoke to his brother. "Because Heaven is the woman that should have been my wife years ago, no matter what I decided later or how I feel now."

CHAPTER TEN

"Hello, roomie."

Heaven cut her eyes at Damen and then focused on the bedroom where Gideon had already dumped his bag and was off to find the game room Damen claimed to have. She took in the wooden four-poster bed, the chandelier overhead, the gleaming hardwood floors, and the silky drapes hanging from the window. "First, it's only for the week, and second"—she gestured to the room—"this doesn't actually scream eleven-year-old boy."

"Yeah, sorry, the house was furnished when I bought it, a foreclosure, and I figured I didn't have anything down here, so why not? Also, Nita already claimed the bedroom next to ours—"

"Yours."

"So, we can get it redone the way Gideon wants. It'll be a cool project between father and son."

"Hm." She hid a smile. "I guess that does sound like a

good idea, but I'm still not your roomie."

"You're staying in my bedroom, aren't you?"

"Only because I suspect you had the furniture removed from the other bedrooms."

He widened his eyes in innocence, but she wasn't falling for it.

"And I don't know why you insist we do this now when the kids have to get to school."

He tugged her into his arms, and she decided not to fight him this time. Damen nuzzled her ear and nipped her earlobe. Goose bumps rose on her skin. "Like I told you we're only about fifteen minutes from your apartment. I can just as easily get Gideon to school from here as you can from over there."

"But."

"Don't say but, Heaven. We will make this work for them and for us."

"For us?"

He kissed along her throat, and she chewed her bottom lip attempting not to moan. "Yes, I'm a good catch, so you should try to make me happy."

"What?" She broke away, but he caught her hand.

"Your money…"

"Has nothing to do with it." The bum put her hand on his cock and wiggled his eyebrows behind his glasses. "Do you know what I can do with this? Very good catch."

She burst out laughing, and he frowned.

"Why are you laughing?"

She glanced around her to make sure they were alone. The beeps and booms of video games sounded from somewhere inside the house, along with Gideon and Nita arguing. "Because you think I should swoon over your dick. I can have you on your knees for this right here."

She pointed to her pussy, and Damen's eyes glazed over. "I don't believe you. Get naked and see if I fall to my knees."

"No way." She ran down the hall past his room. He caught her, hauled her off her feet, and carried her back to his domain. When he kicked the door shut, she protested. "I know you don't think I'm having sex with you, Damen. Gideon or Nita could come here at any time."

"I locked the door."

"They need supervising."

"They're okay until I finish proving my point."

"You don't have a point."

He dumped her on the bed, and she rolled over to scowl at him. The tent in his pants arrested her gaze, and she licked her lips. "My point," he repeated. Heaven rolled her eyes.

When she slid to the edge of the bed, Damen pushed her shoulders and followed her down until she lay flat and he stretched on top of her. His hard-on slid between her legs like her pussy was a homing beacon. If they weren't both dressed, she knew he'd be inside her by now.

Damen stroked her cheek and turned her head gently to face him. "Are you saying you'll deny a poor man all week long? I have to sleep beside you, smelling you, hearing your moans and not be able to touch you?"

"When exactly would I be moaning?"

He chuckled. "In my dreams."

"Luring you to your doom?"

"Correct."

His hand slid along her thigh, and she found herself raising her leg so he could explore a little more. Talk about denying him. Once he touched her, she didn't have much willpower to say no. Besides, she had agreed to come knowing what it might lead to.

Damen's fingers brushed her pussy through her skirt and panties, and she shut her eyes. He kissed along her chest until he reached the valley between her breasts then moved to bite her nipple through her bra.

Heaven's pussy clenched. "Damen, you shouldn't do that."

"Why not? You like it, baby."

She couldn't lie. She did, but Damen didn't hurt her. Just the opposite. His tender touch made her desperate for more of him. He moved farther down her body, but she pushed at his shoulders, drawing in a breath, and tried to steady herself. Damen stilled and looked up at her.

"Heaven?"

She stared at the ceiling. Damen rolled away and stood. She sat up, surprised. "You're leaving?"

"I want to make love to you, but I don't want to push you into what you don't want."

He started for the door, and she sprang to her feet to dart after him. Pressing against his back, she brought her hands around his waist and flattened her palms on his abs. Heaven dipped her head and shut her eyes as she recalled how good he looked naked. He talked about dreaming of her, but she did the same with him. Damen hadn't left her head asleep or awake since well before she moved to New Orleans.

"I'm nervous about getting caught," she admitted.

Damen let her hold him and didn't try to turn around. "We're not doing anything wrong."

"I know, and I don't feel like we are. It's just that I don't want to get it wrong. You seem so relaxed about everything. I'm a ball of knots."

He moved one of her hands to his chest, and she felt it

pounding against her palm. "Don't mistake my joking around for this whole experience being easy for me."

"I'm sorry. I didn't mean it that way."

He spun about and cupped her face between both hands. "I was used to fighting for what I wanted, working around the clock to get it if necessary, but a fight is still a fight."

She nodded. "You used to suggest we stay up half the night studying."

"And you took me from my studies with that body."

"Please, the way I remember it, you wouldn't focus on the material unless I read it to you while sitting on your lap."

He shrugged. "Motivation."

"You passed English Lit, but it had nothing to do with me."

"Woman, you took me to Heaven on a daily basis. It had everything to do with you."

She lowered her gaze, and Damen turned her again to snuggle against her from behind. He pinched open the button on her skirt and lowered the zipper. When he pushed a hand inside her panties, she gasped in pleasure. His fingertips brushed her clit, and the tiny bud swelled. Damen circled it with a gentle touch and eased lower to part her folds.

"Damen."

"If you want me to stop, tell me, Heaven. Touching you drives me nuts, and the sounds you make even more so. Like this." He dipped two fingers inside of her. Heaven squeaked with ecstasy. He growled low in his throat. "Do it again."

He brought the moans forth with the way he massaged her mound. The heel of his hand caressed her while at the same time he pushed fingers in and out of her pussy. She was so wet, he had easy entry, and she couldn't help spreading her legs wider and grinding her butt into his groin.

"I don't want you to stop, but…"

"No buts."

"Damen." His name left her lips as more of a cry of pleasure than a protest to stop. Even if half of Marquette's was downstairs, she wanted this. She wanted him. Damen knew how to play her body and bring her to the edge of an orgasm within seconds of his first touch. He kept stroking her pussy until her legs shook, and she had to hold onto him to keep standing. Her core muscles contracted, and she arched her hips back and pushed forward, driving his fingers deeper. She grabbed his wrist. "W-wait."

Right away, Damen's hand stilled. "What's wrong? I didn't hurt you, did I?"

She smiled at the concern in his tone. "No. Let's go over to the bed. I want you inside me."

His dick twitched against her butt at the mere mention of it. Heaven slid from his arms and tugged him to follow. Damen's gaze was on her rear, and the front of his pants looked like it poked out even more. She needed to help him get more comfortable.

At the bedside, Heaven unbuckled Damen's belt, and he watched with his hands on her hips. She squeezed the button open and lowered the zipper. When she pushed his pants over his narrow hips, she moaned at his cock springing free. Rather than let her completely undress him, he kept his pants and boxers low on his hips and found a condom. When he had it in place, he tapped her butt.

"Take off your panties for me, baby."

Since she still wore her skirt too, she just lifted it and pulled her panties down. Damen couldn't even see anything, but he hissed as if knowing what she did was enough to drive him crazy. Heaven leaned on the bed for balance, and her butt brushed his thigh. Damen jerked her skirt higher so he could see. She slid her panties down her legs and let them land on the floor.

Damen ran his hands up the outsides of her thighs to her hips. "Climb on your knees. I want to see your pussy open for me."

She did, dressed from the waist up, and leaned around to look at him. His green gaze glittered as he stared. She imagined her cootchie was wide open and soaking wet. He kept looking, and she wriggled her hips.

"Damen."

He blew out a noisy breath. "Heaven, what you do to me." He set the tip of his cock to her entrance and gave a tiny shove. She keened, her head falling back. He leaned over her and caressed her cheek and stroked the column of her neck with a featherlight touch. "Easy. From today, this is yours, and you have the right to take it whenever you want."

She shut her eyes, and tears filled them. Arching deep, she took every inch as his dick slid farther. When she was full, he began a slow pump, all the way out and then all the way in. Heaven clutched the sheets. She dropped her chin to her chest and let the tears fall. Damen made slow, aching, and desperate love to her, and the more he took her, the more she loved him.

"Oh, hell," he groaned. "I can't hold it. I wanted... damn..."

She felt him come, and he apologized.

"Way too soon. Don't worry. I'll make you come again and again."

Heaven said nothing. One, she knew he would without him saying so, and two, she was still too choked up. Damen pulled out of her, and she heard the snap of him discarding the condom. The crackle of another wrapper, but he only readied it. She climbed up the bed, hiding her face from him. For a few moments, he stood at the bedside, working his shaft. She knew what would help him along and opened her blouse and yanked up her bra. Heaven didn't have to look to know his gaze was locked on her movements as she pinched and played with her nipples.

He crawled forward and drew her to him with one hand, his mouth homing in on her right breast. Heaven gave a soft cry when he sucked on the stiff peak and let it pop from between his lips. She arched into him, wanting more. At last, his shaft was ready, and he rolled the condom on. Rather than lay on top of her, he drew her up as he sat back. She ended up on his lap, and he guided her down onto his cock.

Heaven hung her arms over Damen's shoulders and buried her face against his neck. They moved in a rhythm that had her pussy buzzing and her insides melting. Another tear fell, but she made sure it landed on her hand and not on his skin.

"You're so quiet, baby," he said into her ear. "I better try harder."

"No, it's good, Damen." She hoped she didn't sound too emotional, and to distract him, she reached under her butt and touched his balls with the tips of her fingers. Damen shuddered. She licked his skin and gave it a tiny nip, and he grunted.

Damen slowed their movements and reached between them to find her clit. She forgot what she was doing from the first massage, and then he made tiny circles on the swollen bud. Her fingernails dug into his shoulders. She whimpered his name.

"That's more like it," he murmured. "Give me more.

Come for me, Heaven."

"Yes!"

The climax sent a pulse through her entire body, robbing her of sense. A sharp scream bubbled in her throat. Damen anticipated it and clapped a hand over her mouth. She rocked on top of him harder and faster than she remembered doing before, all the while shouting behind his hand.

When the bliss ended, Heaven collapsed on his chest. He rubbed her back. "Okay if I keep moving?"

She made a small sound of agreement. He began an unhurried pump, holding her in place with both hands on her butt. They swayed together almost like a dance but quiet, gentle lovemaking.

Heaven lay in bed alone. The room was dark, and she was naked beneath the sheets. The kids were in bed after a long, challenging day. She shifted positions and tensed a little at the soreness between her legs. She and Damen didn't do it rough, but his appetite led to so many sessions, in the end, she was exhausted and a bit achy. She didn't mind because the man knew how to do her body right.

She yawned and stretched. The door opened, and Damen strode in carrying two bowls. She sat up, eager. "Did you get me a mix of butter pecan and chocolate swirl?"

He chuckled. "Yes, you only told me ten times."

"Nine. Don't be dramatic."

He laughed again and handed her the treat. She stuck her spoon into the creamy concoction and pulled up a giant helping. The sweetness touched her tongue, and she moaned in satisfaction.

"No, we're not doing that," Damen said. "You're resting."

"Doesn't your dick need rest too?"

"It's been cocooned in the softest, warmest place on earth. How could it need rest?"

"You like to exaggerate."

"I speak only the truth."

"Uh-huh."

For a while, they sat side by side in a semi-dark room eating ice cream. Heaven wondered where the ice cream calories would begin to settle on her body, and then she thought of Damen. What was he thinking? He had in essence said from now on his body belonged to her, and it had made her cry harder. On the surface, his words sounded warm and wonderful, but she couldn't help realizing that what would have been better was if he had said from now on, his heart was hers. Just thinking it, made hers constrict and tears wet her lashes.

She blinked away the wetness and swallowed the emotion, glad he couldn't see her face very well.

"Heaven."

She froze. "Yeah?"

Damen's spoon clinked against his bowl, and he set it on the bedside table. "I didn't push to know about your dad and you, but if it's not too much for you, I'd like you to tell me about your relationship with him."

She knew it would come at some point. He'd said last week they would talk about it, and they had discussed her mother a little. Her mother and dad had divorced when she was ten, and Heaven had begged to be able to stay with her dad. She and her mom were never close, and Heaven hadn't talked to her in years.

Now she learned Damen hadn't forgotten that they never discussed her dad, but as usual, he was thinking of her feelings. In some ways, Damen was too giving, too accommodating of others. She wondered if that was why his wife had left him and why he let Nita do what she wanted. Damen seemed like he needed someone to balance him out. Then she chided herself, because it sounded like she as trying to convince herself she was the woman for him.

Now who's being selfish?

"You probably don't remember," she began, "but there's this half inch scar on my forehead. It's almost invisible, and my hair covers it most of the time."

"Right here." His fingers went right to it in the dark.

"Great, thanks. You're saying my flaws are glaring."

"No, I just noticed every part of you, and I've spent a lot of time enjoying myself as I looked into your face."

"Oh." She curled her toes under the sheet. With the A/C going and the ice cream, goose bumps popped out on her skin. Damen took her empty bowl and set it atop his. Then he laid back and drew her into his arms.

"Go on."

"When I was a kid, my dad and I argued like cats and dogs. I don't know why we didn't get along. Maybe because I thought I knew everything, or because in a lot of ways I was just like him."

"Hm, I can see that."

She stiffened because she didn't want to believe she was anything like the man now. Damen rubbed her arm, and she let the attitude go. "Anyway, one day, when I was twelve, I must have pushed him farther than I ever did before. I don't remember what I said, but the next thing I knew he had slapped me."

"No!"

"Yeah, don't get me wrong, my dad had never spanked

me before that. Ever. He's the kind of man that will argue with you until you don't care what your point was, if he'd just let it go."

"I can see that too." This time, Damen didn't laugh. She sensed his pent up emotions at hearing about her dad hitting her. He must know since she mentioned the scar, there was more to the story than a slap.

She hesitated because every time she thought of her past, the pain was there choking her. One would think she'd grow indifferent, but she never did. In some ways, she hated him. In others, it was like she still kept stupidly hoping. When she moved to New Orleans, it was during one of those times when she felt strong enough to let that hope go. As she lay beside Damen, she wondered if she was being real with herself.

"The force of the slap made me stumble, and one of my dad's reference books was stacked with some others on the floor. I fell over them, and before I could catch myself, I banged my forehead on the edge of his desk. Cut my skin just like that."

She snapped her fingers, and Damen cried out in alarm.

"It wasn't that big a deal. You know how head wounds bleed more."

"Yeah."

"Well, it was messy. My dad rushed me to the hospital, and they used those butterfly bandages to hold it closed. Not even a stitch. Nothing but that tiny scar."

Damen squeezed her closer to him. "I'm guessing the emotional damage was worse."

"Yes. He never touched me again. No slap, no hug, no nothing. He's cold as ice to me now. Maybe he feels like I did something to him."

"I'm so sorry, Heaven." He shook his head and ran fingers through his hair as he stared up at the ceiling. "I can't reconcile the man you're telling me about with the mentor who has—"

He broke off, and she raised her head. "Damen?"

He laced his fingers with hers. "I've been in contact with him all these years. I considered him a friend, but I realized not more than two or three times did he mention you and never by name. I never made the connection. My head must have been far up my ass."

"Don't blame yourself. It's all him." She sounded bitter, but she couldn't suppress it. "I just wish…"

She gasped and snapped her lips together. Tears gathered. *Damn it, no. Not now.* Too late, she started to cry. Damen engulfed her in his arms and rocked her like a child. She clung to him sobbing. For the moment, he was her lifeline, and she needed his strength. He didn't say anything. He just let her cry until the emotions, which were cresting out of control, died down, and she lapsed into a few hiccupped sighs.

"I don't want to talk about him anymore." She accepted the tissue he offered her from the bedside table.

"Okay."

"Suffice it to say, our relationship stinks, and you already know how he told me basically I'm not good enough for you."

"Fuck him."

"Damen."

"Fuck him, Heaven." He stroked her cheek. "You're going to be my wife, and your dad doesn't enter into that equation. We can get Creed to give you away."

He grinned, and she burst out laughing. "Oh, yeah, I see that happening."

He shrugged. "I've got a way with the beast."

"You're crazy. We haven't seen each other in over a decade. We're clearly different people—or at least you are—and there's no guarantee it would work out between us."

"You're saying if we had known each other all these years, we would have a guarantee?"

"No, of course not. I'm just saying the odds would be better."

"The odds are perfect. We're going to do this. I see it more now than ever."

"I can't figure out your mind."

He kissed her. "That's what will make me a fantastic husband. Okay, sleep. We have two kids that drain every ounce of our energy tomorrow if today was any indicator."

As if on cue, Heaven yawned and covered her mouth. "Don't I know it. All right. Good night."

"Good night, Heaven."

CHAPTER ELEVEN

Heaven couldn't believe the name on the caller ID. In fact, she wondered how Shada had even gotten ahold of her number. Then again, she might have just gone into Creed's office and looked through the employee files. Not like anyone would question his on again off again fiancée. Were they back on now? She answered the phone to find out.

"Hello?"

"This is Shada. I want to talk to you."

Talk about attitude problem. Her tone of voice got Heaven's hackles up, and while she didn't make a habit of mouthing off to people, she couldn't help herself in this instance. "I'll check my schedule to see if I can fit you in. Whoops, look at that. I can't."

"Are you serious?" Shada snapped over the line. "So what, everybody was right about you?"

"I'm not sure how me refusing to talk to you proves anything about what others think about me."

Shada grunted. "Just give me five minutes. I want to know for myself what's going on, not what's rumored around Marquette's."

Heaven felt no compulsion whatsoever to meet with Shada and satisfy her curiosity, but she found herself agreeing anyway. Rather than sort through her thoughts trying to read her motivations, she went with it.

"Gideon's in school until three, but then I have to pick him up. If you've got time before that, fine."

"I'll make the time. Someone can cover for me. How about Café du Monde? Want to meet there?"

"Whatever. One thirty?"

"Sounds good."

Heaven spent the morning nervous as hell about the meeting with Shada. She couldn't concentrate on work and ended up feigning sickness sooner than she intended to. The college she worked for on the West Bank was far enough from the café that she had to catch a bus, and when she left the campus, she just made it to the stop on time. Damen had pushed for her to get a bodyguard, but she had informed him she had no intention of having her steps dogged by some Neanderthal who lived to crack skulls. In truth, she had gotten to know Guy enough to know he wasn't depraved, but because he protected Damen she was forced to get to know him better.

As she got off the bus, she thought of Damen's other, more important suggestion. He called it a suggestion. She called it emotional blackmail, but she understood where he was coming from. Damen wanted Gideon to attend a private school, the same one Nita attended, where security was much tighter. Right now, they took Gideon to school and picked him up. The two of them together had spoken with the principal about Gideon, and no one, including their son, wanted the boy to have a personal bodyguard sitting in the classroom with him. Talk about ruining his chances to make genuine friends.

None of it seemed real since she came from a middle class background, but the sooner she decided the better. The school year had just begun, and they were in a brand new city. Gideon hadn't made close friends yet or gotten used to the school. Still, did she really have to yank him out and put him with rich kids? What if Damen changed his mind and withdrew from Gideon's life? Common sense told her Gideon was his son no matter what. If one day, they stopped growing closer—which would break her and her son's heart—people with bad intentions wouldn't care. Gideon was Damen's. Period.

Heaven passed in front of the café's window and spotted Shada on the other side. Butterflies stirred in her stomach, but she raised her chin and opened the door. A pastry and a cup of coffee sat before Shada, but it looked like she had left off consuming either.

"I got here early," she explained. "You can grab something if you want. I'll wait."

"No, I'm fine." Heaven's appetite had vanished as soon as the café came into view. She sat across from Shada. "What do you want to know?"

"First the obvious. Is Gideon Damen's?"

"Yes."

"How do we know that?"

"*We* don't need to know it. Damen does. I do."

"Do you have proof?" The interrogation was beginning to rankle Heaven's nerves.

"I'll be glad to let Damen get a paternity test if he asks

for one. He hasn't."

Distracted, Shada took a sip of the coffee and frowned. "Crap, I let it get cold. Well, I'm used to Marquette's food, and I guess I'm partial either way."

"Yeah, I bet."

Shada eyed her.

"Rumor has it you're playing games with Creed, or is it back on with you two?"

"I'm not playing games with him! You don't know anything about me."

Heaven tilted her head to the side. "Oh, that's funny because you seemed happy enough to pretend you know me. And you thought it was fine to call me out here questioning me about something that's none of your business."

"When it comes to Creed, it is my business. We might have our issues, but I love him. He's worried about Damen, and that makes me worry about him. I figured as a woman, I could feel you out and see if you're the gold-digger Creed thinks you are."

"Maybe you're the gold-digger," Heaven pushed through clenched teeth. "Anybody can say they love someone, and you wouldn't be the first."

"I'm not on trial."

"Neither am I!"

Shada sat back and folded her arms over her chest. "This is all about Damen and his son. You're getting nothing out of it?"

Heaven sighed. "I'm tired of justifying myself to you. Why are you tormenting Creed?"

"Excuse me?"

Heaven leaned forward. "You heard me. When I worked at Marquette's, I saw the way he looked at you. I would give—

He had this look like…I don't know. He loves you a lot. That's rare, and you need to think about it. If he loves you even half as much as I think he does, it's killing him to be apart from you. Every day he has to wake up alone."

The fire had gone out of Shada's eyes, but she tried to dredge it up again and failed. "You don't know what I've been through."

"No, I don't, but I know what Creed's been through."

Shada brown eyes blazed in anger. "Excuse me?"

"Their dad used to hit Creed, and he took it to protect his brothers. You said he's worried about Damen. Creed had to stand at the top and take the abuse. His mother wasn't there for him, and Damen and Stefan couldn't help him the way he needed it. Who does he have now, Shada? You? No, you're too busy jerking him around running away, and worrying about whatever it is in your own past. Do you know how much it kills a person to have someone you love reject you?"

"You had someone do that?" Shada said in a low voice.

Heaven heaved a sigh. "It doesn't matter. Gideon is Damen's. To bring peace to their family, I'm going to push Damen to take the paternity test. Then maybe Creed will back off, but you should concentrate on yourself."

Heaven stood and turned away, but Shada grabbed her arm. "Wait, you're really going to do that?"

"Yeah, why not? It's what you all want, isn't it?"

Shada smiled for the first time. "Well, I guess if it was me, I'd tell everybody to kiss my ass and I'm not proving anything. Unless of course it would mean the difference between getting what my son needed and not. Listen to me. Now I sound like I'm on your side. From where you stand, you don't have to prove it. Damen is offering you a lot more than just child support."

"Oh, you heard that too? Yes, he asked me to marry him."

"Damen and I have never gotten along, but I hear his ex-wife hurt him bad. If you're expecting to seduce him into falling in love with you, girlfriend, forget it. I think his heart is still taken."

Heaven swung away, putting her back to Shada. "I know."

She started forward, but Shada caught her again and walked around to block her path. "Oh damn, you love him, don't you? You actually love that fool Damen. Who'da thunk it?"

"I respect—"

"Save it, girl." Shada waved her hand. "Your secret is out, and now that I'm not angry anymore, I can see it written all over your face."

"Thanks. You're all heart."

Shada grinned. "Well, I still don't want to get married, but hey, I'm not against other people doing it if they feel it's right for them. He asked you. Why don't you do it? You get to enjoy the man you love. I can't say how it will go because for real, Damen is weird. I don't know anyone who gets the way his mind works. You might be happy, even if it lasts for one day."

"Right back at you."

Shada shook her head. "Different circumstances all together."

"If you say so."

They walked together outside to the street, and Heaven couldn't say they had become friends in that short amount of time. They did understand each other a little better. Who knew if it would stick after Shada talked to Creed again. Despite Creed's attitude toward her, she hoped it would work between him and Shada.

"Let me give you a ride," Shada offered when a car pulled up to the curb, and she strode over to it.

Heaven peered through the windshield, another big guy, less threatening than Guy, but he didn't give her the warm and fuzzies either. She recognized him as Creed's bodyguard, Pete. Shada must be borrowing him while Creed was at the restaurant. She seemed to take it in stride, but then again, she had been with Creed longer.

"No, thank you. I'm fine."

Shada scanned the area with a frown. "Are you sure?"

"Positive. Please tell Creed he doesn't have to worry about Damen when it comes to me. None of you do." Before Shada could say more, she turned on her heel and strode off. She would keep her word, and there wasn't a doubt in her mind she could convince Damen to take the test and put everybody's mind to rest.

Some of the family would probably still see her as an opportunist, but so what. So long as Damen knew the truth, and Gideon was happy. What the others thought of her didn't matter.

Rather than head back to her apartment or take a taxi to Damen's house, Heaven decided to walk over to the French Market, which wasn't that far. She headed under the arch and along the aisle of vendors sharing their wares on either side of her. A table caught her attention, covered with a red cloth and atop that stacks of small alligator heads. Heaven cringed.

"They're real," the seller assured her and held up one as if she cared. Heaven tried to force a polite smile, but it stuck, and she spun away.

Um, hell no.

She moved on the to the grate with fuzzy masks attached to it and ran a fingertip over the soft creations. The "aww" she was about to utter died at the skull masks next to the kitty ones. That was New Orleans, she figured.

Heaven was about to continue on to the area where she could buy fruit when someone grabbed her arm from behind. She looked around, and went cold.

"Did you think I would give up, Heaven?"

She tried to tug her arm away and failed. "Why are you still here, Leon?"

He sneered. "Why do you think? To get you to come to your senses."

"I don't need to come to my senses. We're done, and I told you so before I left."

"You mean over text while you were on the plane?"

"For my own safety because you don't know how to keep your hands to yourself." She pulled at her arm. "Get off me, Leon."

"Or what?" He leaned closer, and she bent backward away from him. His hold tightened.

"Young man, can't you see this lady doesn't want you bothering her?"

They both turned to see an old woman at least eighty glaring at Leon. He flared his nostrils. "Back off, Grandma, before you get hurt. This is my girlfriend, and we're having a conversation."

Heaven shoved at his chest, which did nothing, and he spun on his heel to propel her back through the arch. The crowd swallowed the old lady, and Heaven looked around for anybody that might help. No one seemed to notice, but she didn't expect them to, and she didn't cry out because fear shut her throat. She was used to Leon's manhandling and threatening her to keep her mouth shut.

Leon shoved her toward a bench at the end of the

pavilion. "Sit down."

Heaven hesitated, but he squeezed her shoulder and forced her downward. Her knees gave, and she dropped onto the bench. She blinked over and over and chewed her bottom lip while staring straight ahead. Leon sat beside her, and she felt his angry gaze.

"You better not cry," he threatened. "I had to chase you all the way down here and take time off from work. It's not easy to find something else here either."

She gaped at him. "You're not moving to New Orleans?"

"Why not? You're here." He grasped her arm again and held it too tight in his meaty grip. "Heaven, you know I love you, right? Come on, girl, we're good together. Forget that dumbass white guy. You messed up getting with him years ago, but you were young and stupid then. Stay with your own kind—me."

"Human is my own kind," she quipped before she caught herself. "It has nothing to do with the color of my skin."

He pointed a finger in her face, and she braced for a smack. None came. "You like to push me, Heaven, but I'm going to prove how I feel."

She looked at him, scared of what he meant. Surely, he wouldn't do anything to hurt Damen. As Leon dug around in his pockets, rattling keys in his search, she watched him. A slow dread built up in her chest, and she wished more than anything she could go back in time and accept Shada's offer of a ride. If she had, she would be safely behind a locked door by now.

"Got it," Leon declared and pulled his hand from his pocket. Heaven's mouth fell open at the ring with the tiny diamond set in the middle. The piece looked real, and from the pride in Leon's expression, she guessed it was.

"No," she whispered.

He didn't appear to have heard her. Leon grabbed her hand and shoved the ring onto her finger, almost breaking it in the process. Heaven cried out, and the pressure eased, but it didn't stop him from moving the ring over her knuckle and settling it into place.

"Now, we can get married. We talked about it, remember?"

Hypothetical, she thought, before she had gotten a grip, and before the abuse had gotten too bad to endure. Heaven shook her head. She tried to retrieve her hand so she could snatch the ring off, but Leon wouldn't let go. "I told you that's not what I want, Leon. You don't listen to me."

"Because you don't know what you want."

"I know what I want," she insisted, "and it's not you. We broke up."

"No!" He looked over his shoulder, for the first time concerned about someone overhearing. Then he faced her, laying a hand on her jaw. His big hand engulfed her face, suffocating her without covering her mouth. She couldn't breathe for fear and the threat of his violence. Leon would never take it that far in public, but he had hurt her often enough in private he was able to use subtle touches to communicate what would happen later. In that way, he maintained control of her when other people were around.

Heaven didn't move. She imagined to anyone several feet away, she and Leon looked like a happy couple, her man caressing her face and holding her hand. All the old feelings washed over her, and the small ring was a boulder crushing her fingers and her heart.

"Heaven, be realistic. I mean you lived a fantasy for a while, right? Pretending you were going to get with that rich guy, but seriously, why should he be with a black girl like you?"

"There's nothing wrong with me."

"No, you're smart and everything, but a black girl? Maybe to fuck but not to get serious over. So you had his son. Who cares? He probably looks at it like a mistake, and from the way all those people acted at that restaurant, I bet every one of them feels the same way, especially his family."

Heaven blinked.

"Yeah, that's right. I looked them up. The Marquettes." Leon spit on the ground. "What kind of stupid name is that?"

"I love their name."

"Why because you think it's going to be yours? Or hell, your son's?" He laughed. "Wake up. Maybe you're not as smart as I thought you were. If that guy's being nice to you it's because he just wants to fuck you."

Leon appeared ready to destroy something with the thought alone.

"It'll wear off," he growled, "and then you and your son are going to find yourselves on the street. He'll use some high-powered lawyer to force you to back off, like get you fired and your reputation ruined so you can't find work until you sign something that says you'll keep your mouth shut about the kid."

She started to shake. "Damen wouldn't do that."

"What about the other one? What's his name? That mean guy who was at the restaurant. Fuck, even I got a little nervous when he turned all cold and snobby like rich people do."

Heaven didn't say anything. She dropped her chin against her chest, and a tear rolled down her cheek. Leon's hold on her hand tightened, and she gasped.

"I told you don't cry out here," he snapped and squeezed harder. How did he expect her not to cry when he hurt her like this?

"I'm s-sorry."

Leon leaned closer to her, bringing their faces within inches of each other. "I see I'm going to have to take you home and beat your ass for you to learn."

"N-no."

"You didn't just tell me no, did you?"

Words escaped her.

"Is that what you want, Heaven? You want me to beat your ass? You remember, right? Maybe I need to remind you because you've been down here a few weeks, and you got stupid. Your son's in school, so I've got plenty of time."

Make a scene. You're not a victim anymore, Heaven. You're strong. Fight back!

Leon dragged her to her feet, and he shuffled her in the direction of the lot next to French Market. She spotted his car before they reached it. He must have driven down, and even before they reached the vehicle, she caught site of boxes in the backseat. A sense of hopelessness washed over her. He really was planning to move to New Orleans.

At the passenger side of the car, she hung back. "No, I'm not going anywhere with you, Leon, and I don't want your ring."

He had released her hand to remove the car keys from his pocket, and when he did, she started to take off the ring. Leon brought a fist down atop hers and slammed left arm against the side of the car. She cried out. He pressed his length along hers. Bile rose in her throat.

"Try to take that ring off and see what I do, right out here, and I don't care who sees it."

Heaven clutched her arm and sobbed. She was beyond control and past figuring out how to get away. There were no weapons in her purse, and even as she looked down at it, her arm started to swell. Leon banged the flat of a palm on the roof of the car, giving her an eyeful of the massive, tight muscles of his arm. Flexed, his biceps were as big as her head. Mentally, she curled in on herself, but she knew she couldn't get in the car. *Never again.*

"I hate you," she whispered. "I never really hated my dad even after he got me to leave Damen, but I hate you, Leon. I might not be the kind of person that will rise up and fight physically, but I do it in my own way. I'm not going. You're going to have to beat me right here and risk getting caught. I won't ever be with you again."

"Oh, that's how it is?"

She couldn't answer. The strength it had taken to speak had fizzled. Her arm throbbed, and her mind was a jumble. The southern sun beat down, bringing dizziness and nausea. At some point, Heaven realized Leon could just force her in the car and get her to her apartment whether she agreed to go or not.

He raised a fist in front of her face. "You'll change your mind."

She darted to the side. He caught her by her injured arm, and she cried out. The next thing she knew Leon rose off his feet and slammed on the ground. Heaven looked up into Guy's angry face, and the big man dropped to one knee between parked cars. He drove a fist into Leon's jaw, and her ex's head snapped back. Guy dragged him up enough to keep him from cracking the back of his head on the ground and pounded on him a few more times.

Leon's lip split, both eyes shut, and his nose gushed blood. At first Heaven felt a sense of satisfaction, and then her stomach tumbled. She staggered away to the end of the car. "Guy, stop, *please."*

She didn't think he'd heard her, but the pounding ended immediately. A thud reached her, and she assumed Guy had dropped Leon, but she had shut her eyes.

"Ms. Heaven, are you okay?" Guy asked, his voice coming from beside her. She was glad he didn't attempt to touch her.

"No." She swallowed over and over.

Something beeped. Her knees knocked, and she wobbled.

"I can carry you, Ms. Heaven."

"Don't touch me." Her voice was too sharp. She didn't mean it. All she felt for him was gratitude. He had saved her, and she wanted to tell him, but confusion and weariness engulfed her. Not to mention the fact that she still couldn't open her eyes. She imagined she looked like a druggie nodding off after getting high.

After a few moments, Heaven's stomach settled, and she slitted her eyes. The sun seemed brighter, and it hurt. Her arm throbbed. The ring pinched into her skin. The disgusting thing would have to be cut off. Could she manage a step without Guy's help, or would she fall on her face and make an even bigger idiot of herself?

Fresh tears fell down her cheeks. She had thought she was making a new life for her and Gideon, but the old ties wanted to keep her bound. After some moments, she realized Guy was saying something. She focused on his words.

"Ms. Heaven, please don't go anywhere without me anymore. I came to your job to pick you up, but you weren't there. You left early. Please don't do that without telling me. If I offend you, then we can get someone else to watch over you. I actually know a guy who's small, but he gets the job done. I'm sure he won't make you scared."

"Watch over me?" She glanced at him. He stood between

her and Leon, who lay unconscious on the ground. Guy was close enough to catch her if she fell down, but his hands were pressed firmly to his sides. He stood stiff and still, no doubt trying not to look intimidating. If she didn't hurt so much, it would be funny.

"Yes, Mr. Damen told me to watch you, but I was at the restaurant until it was almost time to pick you up. I'm sorry I didn't find you before he hurt you."

She nodded. "Where's your car, Guy? Can you go get it? I don't think I have the energy to move far."

"I can't do that."

"But you don't have to park. You can drive it up this little road here, and I'll get in."

He shook his head. "If you won't let me carry you, we have to wait. I can't leave you again."

She peered at Leon. "He's not getting up any time soon."

Guy said nothing. Heaven was about to try convincing him again to go get the damn car when tires screeched to a halt, and she looked around. A black car had slid to a stop in front of her, and the driver side and passenger side doors flew open. Pete appeared from the passenger seat, and Damen leaped from behind the wheel. He circled the car and beat Pete to Heaven.

"Heaven!" Damen's eyes widened at sight of her arm. His voice dropped to a growl. "Where is he?"

"He's there, sir." Guy pointed, and Damen looked like he would go after Leon for himself, but she clutched his shirtfront. He paused to gaze down at her, concern in his eyes.

"Damen, I'm hurting. I need to sit down."

"You need a doctor." He scooped her into his arms and headed to the car. Guy zipped forward to yank the back door open for them. Damen set her inside and climbed in after. He glanced out at Guy. "Do something with him. We don't need him dying on us."

"Yes, sir."

"Pete, the hospital."

"Sir."

"Damen, I don't need to go to the hospital."

"Hush." He drew her onto his lap, and then he noticed the ring. She tried to hide it, but he gently took her hand in his. "What is this?"

Sickness assailed her all over again. "He forced it on me."

Damen was quiet. She couldn't stand wondering what he thought and was about to ask when he spoke. "The only ring that's going there is mine. We'll get this cut off at the hospital, and it's going in the trash where it belongs. Rest, Heaven. Put your head on my shoulder."

She stiffened. "I have to get Gideon from school."

"I'll take care of it." He patted his chest. "Right here."

She leaned into him and relaxed in the safety of his embrace.

CHAPTER TWELVE

Heaven laid back in Damen's bed, her arm in a sling and her wrist wrapped in a bandage. Both her shoulder and her wrist were sprained, and the doctor had prescribed rest and pain meds. Voices reached her from downstairs, and she climbed out of bed to open the door. Damen wouldn't like it, but she hated lying around. After Gideon had come in to tell her his Uncle Creed of all people had picked him up from school, she had fallen asleep and hadn't gotten a chance to talk to Damen.

Footsteps on the landing sent her stumbling back to bed. The drugs were powerful stuff. She almost catapulted onto her face and had trouble raising a knee up onto the mattress when the door opened.

"Heaven!"

She looked around. Damen stood in the doorway holding a tray. "This isn't what it looks like."

He thumped the tray on the bedside table and raised her

into his arms to lie on the bed. "I told you not to move."

"I was tired of sleeping."

"You slept two hours, and the only reason why you think you can move is the drugs are strong."

"How can I 'think' I'm moving when I'm actually moving?"

Damen's expression was dead serious. She had never seen him like that. "Heaven, you could have been hurt much worse today."

She turned her face from him. "I have been—many times."

"Then after today it never happens again. You'll have your own bodyguard with you at all times."

"Damen, that's not realistic."

"Please." He stroked her hair from her face and pulled the sheets up closer to her chin. "Don't argue with me about it."

"Damen."

"Heaven, I told Gideon you fell."

She gasped. "I don't want him to know the truth. I kept it from him all this time."

"You didn't."

"What?"

He sat on the side of the bed and leaned down to kiss her. "The reason Gideon wants to take self-defense classes is so he can get strong enough to protect you. He talked to me about it, and he asked if I would help him to do it. He said your ex hurt you, and he couldn't do anything to stop it because he was so small and weak."

Heaven started to cry, hearing the pain in Damen's voice and realizing the desperation in her son. "I guess I knew he wasn't fooled, but I didn't want to face it. Leon never hit Gideon, not once. If anything, he ignored Gideon's existence, which was better for him."

Damen nodded.

"Did you tell him it's okay and that I don't need protecting?"

"No, I told him we would both take care of you, and I wouldn't let anyone who would hurt you near enough to do so again."

"Damen."

"I'm serious, Heaven." He caressed her cheek, and she felt only comfort from him. "You get a bodyguard. Guy suggested someone, and I've called him to meet with you. If he doesn't scare you, he's the one."

"Seriously, I'm not some lame woman who can't look out for herself. Leon was an exception. I can stand on my own two feet."

She argued that she could, but in reality, she was terrified she couldn't. Damen ran a fingertip along her ring finger. She knew he hadn't let go of the notion that they get married, and after all that junk Leon had said, she doubted the idea even more.

"I want you to take a paternity test," she said.

"No."

"Why not? It will prove to everyone Gideon's yours, and your family will at least accept him."

"But not you? Is that what you're saying?"

She pressed her lips together.

"I was considering it to get Creed off my back, but no. With time, we'll prove him wrong."

She looked into his eyes. "Wait, Damen. Are you scared Gideon's *not* yours?"

"That's nonsense."

"No, it's not." She thought about it. "Your ex betrayed

you. My dad turned out to not be the man you thought he was, and then there's me coming out of the woodwork after you become rich, why should you believe me? Plus, I could just be using reverse psychology, pretending to want you to get the test but guilting you into not getting it."

He raised an eyebrow in doubt.

"It's possible, Damen."

"All right."

He didn't expound on his agreement, making her think she had called it, and he didn't believe her. The knowledge hurt even if she had no right to expect anything else.

"How about this?" Damen suggested.

"I'll get the test if you agree to marry me, and you have to follow through. No putting it off. You keep your word, and we get married."

She gaped. "That's playing dirty."

"Do we have a deal?"

"Damen, you could live to regret it if you marry me. This would be your second marriage, or have you forgotten?"

"I haven't forgotten, and I'm not going to regret my decision. Do you agree or not?"

She hesitated a minute longer, weighing the options. If she married Damen without getting the test, everyone could go on forever thinking she married him for his money. There would be tension between him and his brothers, maybe forever. Their sour relationship might affect the kids, and all she wanted for Gideon and even Nita was for them to be happy.

If they got the test and of course it was proven that Gideon was Damen's, then if they married, everyone would come to accept her—hopefully. More importantly, they would accept Gideon into their fold. The Marquettes were already a blended race family from what she had seen, so the fact that Gideon was biracial wouldn't be an issue.

A new thought struck Heaven. She had been thinking over her options based on her marrying Damen as if it were a done deal. The fact was, she really wanted to be his wife, and something deep inside wanted to show him she could be a good one.

Damn.

She wanted to lecture herself into letting the image go that popped into her head, of her and Damen at the altar, of the two of them with their kids as a family. Leon hadn't killed the hope in her after all. Her love for Damen and longing to be with him was too strong.

He doesn't love me, she tried to remind herself. Then she thought of Damen showing up at the French Market, angry at Leon and holding her on his lap like she was precious to him. She thought of how Damen had promised their son they would both take care of Heaven. Maybe Damen's feelings stemmed from her being his son's mother and also from the sexual compatibility they shared.

Heaven groaned and rubbed her forehead. Damen leaned closer and took her hand in his. "I'm sorry. I'm pushing you too hard when you're hurt. Eat a little of this food and get some more rest. We can talk about us later."

"No."

"Heaven, you need to eat." His voice was stern but gentle.

"That's not what I mean. We don't have to talk about it later." She swallowed. Her stomach did flip-flops, and if she didn't pass out in the next few seconds, it would be a miracle. "Yes, I'll marry you, *if* you get the paternity test first. And don't worry. I won't go back on my word."

He grinned. "I'd like to add another stipulation."

You're pushing your luck, sir."

He chuckled. "We don't tell the others until one month after our wedding about the test."

"What kind of jimmy john mess is that?"

She smiled at the confusion in his expression at her crazy words. Heaven had heard it a lot from the same crazy friend who she had stolen the "it's because I'm black" joke from.

"Our secret, Heaven," he insisted. "No one knows about the test or the results until well after we're married."

"But then they might not come to the wedding."

"They'll come."

"I don't want you to be hurt."

He grinned. "I won't be. I'm marrying a sexy and beautiful woman, aren't I?"

"I'm more than my body, you know?"

"Yes, I know." He leaned down and pressed his face to her belly and rested one of his hands on her hip. She watched him in awe and confusion as he stayed that way a long while, and then he turned his head to look into her eyes. "I don't pretend to be a perfect man, Heaven."

"You're close to it," she blurted and then blushed in embarrassment.

He had the nerve to look full of himself. "I'm glad my wife thinks so."

"I'm not your wife yet."

"But you will be soon. I'm thinking next week."

She made a strangled sound. "You're insane."

He raised his head to kiss her hipbone through the sheets and then laid it back down on her. The sigh of contentment from him made her wonder. "No, it's not too soon."

"T-the paternity test might take a while, maybe a few weeks."

He frowned. "Do you know that for a fact?"

"No, I never looked into it. I didn't need to."

"Neither have I, but I doubt that's the case. Who knows? It might be a few days turnaround, and we can—"

"Don't even say it. This is my first wedding, and I want it done right. You can't take that away from me."

His eyes widened, and he sat up. "You're right. Whatever you want, but it goes forward immediately. Hire a planner. I'm sure if money isn't an object, she can work miracles within a time constraint."

Heaven groaned. He wouldn't give up on them doing this fast. Well, she knew she wasn't marrying him for money, and he had the means to spend whatever it took. She refused to feel bad about it. This was what Damen insisted he wanted. He would get it, and Gideon would be fine.

"One more thing," Damen said, and she tensed.

"What do you think of me adopting Gideon? Before you say anything, let me explain how it works."

"I know how it works. I did look into that, and yes, that would make me happy. If he can have your name and be yours even on paper, it's perfect."

"Good. Then it's settled."

Settled, he said. Heaven felt like they were just getting started.

Heaven felt weird being back inside Marquette's, especially as a bride-to-be with no waitressing duties to perform. She listened to her wedding planner with only half an ear talking about table positions, settings, and other details. Not that Heaven wasn't interested. She was into her wedding, and with each passing day, she grew more nervous and more excited.

There was also tension, and she feared it would screw up the happiness that bubbled inside her every time Damen looked her way.

While Heaven was glad of her decision to marry Damen, and he showed signs of feeling the same way, there was also Creed's opinion to deal with.

"Don't you think this is a little sudden?" Creed had demanded of Damen when they broke the news.

Damen had shrugged. "Yeah, it is, but it's happening."

Creed had looked at her, his expression dark. Heaven shivered and resisted an urge to hug herself, but Damen had noticed.

"Fix your face, Creed."

Creed started. "What do you me— Look, I'm just thinking of you, Damen. You've dealt with women who weren't…the right one before. I don't want to see you make another mistake."

Heaven forgot her fear. She moved in front of Damen to face Creed, hands on her hips. "You're saying I'm a mistake? *You're* the mistake! Damen should have an older brother who supports him no matter what, not insult his fiancée to his face. If you don't agree with what we're doing, you can get lost. I told Damen we don't have to have the wedding here, and we definitely don't need you!"

Damen's hands came down on her arms, and he drew her to his chest. "Calm down, baby."

She wiggled in his hold, but Damen kept her still. She knew he hid how Creed's attitude affected him, but all the while he hadn't changed his mind. The only way she had gotten the man to slow down was in asking him to wait for her shoulder and wrist to heal. He'd agreed in a heartbeat and apologized for being insensitive. They took the paternity test in secret, and of course it showed Damen was Gideon's father. No man had ever flown higher than Damen that day, and she had to curb his crazy behind from spoiling Gideon like he had done with Nita. So nobody knew better than her what he must feel to have Creed still standing against them. Heaven had begged Damen to tell the truth, but he reminded her of their agreement each time.

"See my half-pint defender?" Damen joked to Creed.

Heaven glared over her shoulder at him. "Who's a half-pint?"

He ignored her, his focus on Creed. "If you don't want us to have the wedding here, we won't."

Creed shrugged, his anger fading to indifference. "Marquette's is partly yours."

"Then if you don't want to come…"

Creed's gaze flew to Damen, and his eyes widened. "Are you saying you don't want me here?"

"No, of course not. I want my brothers here with me and Heaven." Damen shifted against Heaven's back, and she knew what was coming—more evidence the man was bonkers. "In fact—"

"Damen," she interrupted, jittery. "You don't need to—"

"I'd like you to give Heaven away, Creed."

The office where they stood at that moment was silent as a tomb. Creed stared at Damen. Damen stared back, and Heaven was wound so tight, the strings of her mental faculties were about to pop. She licked her lips and drew in a steadying breath, which did zip to pull her together. Damen's hands slid up to her shoulders to give them a gentle squeeze.

He continued. "She doesn't have family who can support her or that she wants here. Her friends are coming, but I suggested you."

"Why me?" Creed frowned. "She's not mine to give to you."

"It's ceremony, a symbol."

Creed ground his teeth.

"But if you're not coming, then we can think of someone else," Damen finished.

Heaven wanted to look into his face, but he was holding her too close to see now, standing behind her. His voice sounded steady enough, but she couldn't be sure.

"Don't be stupid," Creed snapped. "I'm not going to miss your wedding. Contrary to what some feel about me"—he glared at Heaven—"I've never not been with you and Stefen, in *everything*, even when I didn't like what you were up to."

Damen chuckled. "That's true, and we've dragged you into a lot. This shouldn't be anything new."

"It's not!" Creed scratched the back of his head. "Let me think about this other thing."

"By all means, bro. I'm expecting you to do it."

Creed swore. "You're a pushy bastard."

"Yes, I am," Damen said proudly. "Good, that's settled. I've got a couple things to attend to." He turned Heaven to face him and kissed her lips. Creed left the office. Heaven nuzzled closer into Damen's arms and shut her eyes.

"Are you sure about this, Damen?"

"We've been over it. It's the only way to force Creed out of his shell."

"I wasn't aware he was in one."

"Yeah, no one knows my brother like I do."

"Shada might have a thing or two to say about that."

He raised her chin. "Trust me?"

She studied his face. "Yes, I do."

"Good. Now, I have a couple things to check out. Do

you want me to take you home?"

"No, I'll stay longer, and I have my new bodyguard here." She had met the man who was not much taller than she was and who was wiry, but she sensed strength about him. His alert gaze said he saw everything that was happening around them, and he had come highly recommended by Guy. Best of all, Weaver didn't scare the crap out of her with height and bulk, so he worked.

"Okay, but no leaving Marquette's without him. Agreed?"

"I don't feel the need to show my independence by being stupid. I'll keep him with me."

"Good girl." He kissed her and hugged her tighter. "I'll call you."

She nodded and watched him go. Heaven checked her messages and found a couple texts from the planner. She answered the questions as she left the office and then paused in the hallway at a sound coming from the bathroom. A knock on the door produced nothing, and she tried the doorknob to find it locked.

"Hello?" she called though the door. "Are you okay in there?"

At first there was no answer, and then the lock clicked, the door swung open, and she was dragged inside. Shada slammed the door again and winced. Heaven stared at her. Shada's eyes were red and wet as if she had been crying, and she looked pale.

Heaven frowned. "I thought you and Creed were back together. Did you break up again?"

"No." Shada spun away to the sink and washed her face. Heaven handed her a few paper towels, and Shada mopped her forehead. "We still have our issues, and we fight like cats and dogs, but..."

"But what?"

Shada moaned.

Heaven walked over to her and touched a hand to the woman's back. They weren't friends, but since that talk at the café, they weren't enemies either. Heaven had spoken with Shada a handful of times on the phone during the planning of her wedding. Shada had agreed to make the cake, and Marquette's was catering.

"What is it?" Heaven pressed.

"I screwed up," Shada said. "I screwed up big time."

"How?"

Shada met her gaze in the mirror. "I think I'm pregnant."

"Whoa! How awesome. Congratulations."

"No, it's not awesome." Tears spilled down Shada's cheeks. "It's terrible. I'm…I don't want…I'm freaking scared. What if something happens to me?"

"You mean because of your age? Just eat right, get rest, and don't miss any of your doctor's visits."

"You sound like a commercial," Shada complained. "You don't know my issues. I lost my parents when I was young. It about killed me. Then I had a sister. She died last year. I vowed I wouldn't love anyone else and risk getting hurt. If I lose the baby, or if it's born… All kinds of thoughts are running through my head, chief of all, why the hell didn't I make sure the pills were working right after I went back on them before I spread my legs for Creed?"

"Um, okay. Well, what's done is done. You're having his baby, and the fear will at some point be taken over by the love. I know from experience. Just grin and bear it."

Shada flared her nostrils. "You suck at advice."

"You just don't want to hear the truth."

Shada moaned again. "I'm still really early. Maybe I

should—"

Heaven didn't say a word, but she knew just what was on Shada's mind. She was considering an abortion, and Heaven, who considered children to be gifts wasn't hearing it. She knew what she'd said was true. From what Shada had said, Shada wasn't against kids. Her fears were just so big she couldn't see around them. Heaven believed without a doubt in her mind that little infant would cure Shada in a heartbeat. If nothing else, she would do everything in her power to stay well for the baby, so she could be around until the baby was grown.

"Are you feeling sick?" Heaven asked.

"No, I just know my body, and something wasn't right. I suspected it, so I took a test. It came out positive."

"If you want, we can sit down and talk about it. I can tell you some of what to expect."

Shada's chin dipped to her chest. "I'm not ready to come out of this bathroom. I might move in here."

Heaven laughed. "Let me get you a bottled water."

"Make it alcohol."

"Water," Heaven repeated and left the bathroom. She didn't think twice about her decision. Shada needed help, and if she wasn't forced at this point to move past her issues, she wouldn't. Later, she would regret a bad choice made out of fear. Heaven had acted on fear for years—or *didn't* act because of it—and that had gotten her into trouble. Well, she would do what she could for Shada, even if they ended up as sisters-in-law but never friends.

Heaven moved by the arriving kitchen staff for their afternoon and night shift, and headed out to the dining room. Weaver stood near the front entrance, chatting with Pete. Heaven caught their attention. "Creed?"

Weaver pointed toward the ceiling, and Heaven swung away to head up the back stairs. The second floor held the second biggest dining room with double French doors leading into it. These stood open, and Heaven walked in to find Creed discussing something with one of the waiters. She figured someone had reserved the room for a private party, which happened pretty often. Marquette's was the best restaurant in New Orleans. Heaven was glad that in marrying Damen she wouldn't have to lose access to such a great place. Marquette's, in the short time she had worked there, felt like a part of her family.

"Can I talk to you?" she asked Creed and stood quiet while the waiter left. Creed narrowed his eyes. "If you're up here to pressure me about giving you away, you can just wait until I'm ready to give you my decision."

"It's not about me." She wanted to tell him it wasn't about him either, maybe dump him off his high horse, but that would be silly. "It's about Shada."

He stiffened. "What about her?"

Heaven watched for his reaction. "She's pregnant."

Creed paled. "What?"

"She's pregnant, I said. Right now, she's in the bathroom downstairs, probably wondering why I'm taking so long to come back."

Creed took a second to confirm she was serious, and then he tore off toward the stairs. From the racket he made, she figured he either rolled down the stairs or jumped down every other one.

"What's going on?" someone shouted, coming into the hall.

"Move," Creed bellowed and must have thrust through them all. Heaven grinned. Shada might be mad at her, but it wouldn't last. Whether Creed would drive Shada crazy from then until the baby was born was the real question.

Heaven took her time descending the stairs. When she reached the bottom, all lay in silence. She decided whatever she intended to do at the restaurant could wait, and she had Weaver drive her home. They were only halfway there when Damen called.

"Didn't you just leave?" she asked when she answered.

"I wanted to let you know I just talked to Creed. He said Shada's pregnant and that you were the one to tell him."

"Ah. Did he sound happy?"

"Delirious. My brother was almost intolerable when he and Shada broke it off. I have a feeling she's going to kill him before the baby is born."

"Why do you say that?"

"Because the bear is now a daddy. He's going to be overprotective."

Heaven laughed. "I'll bet. Poor girl."

"Well, now he tells me he'll do whatever you want. He'll give you away. He'll dance and sing at our wedding."

Heaven winced. "Okay."

"See what I told you? He's deliriously happy, and it's all because of you, beautiful." His voice dropped low, and she got the impression he was happy too and put the reason at her feet.

"I can't take credit. He did the 'work.'"

Damen chuckled. "I guess you're right. I need to go. Can you take care of picking up the kids today?"

"Nita too?" She was surprised. "Am I on the list to get her?"

"Yes, I added you a couple days ago."

She had done the same for him before Gideon had been

transferred to the new private school. After her ordeal with Leon, she didn't want her son's safety to ever be an issue, but they had picked up the kids together before today.

"Okay, that's fine," she said.

"I might be a little late."

"What are you doing, Damen? I know you're not at Marquette's."

"Later," he insisted.

"Fine."

They both rang off, and Heaven realized she had been close to ending the call with "I love you." She wondered if there would ever come a time when saying it would be the norm for them. Or would they continue as friends and lovers for years as their kids grew up together. Being Damen's friend wasn't a bad deal, except that loving him made it harder and left her unsure. As she thought of what Shada had shared of her life, she considered she was doing what was right for herself and for Gideon. Even if her love was unrequited, it was far better to love someone deeply than to love no one for fear of loss.

I love Damen. Admitting it to herself felt good and somewhat satisfying. In that moment, she decided, she would admit it to him and shower him with all she had in her heart to give.

CHAPTER THIRTEEN

"Girl, breathe," Jada demanded, studying Heaven's face in the mirror. "If you pass out, I think I'm going to join you. Then what's going to happen?"

"Daddy will stop being a blinking robot," Nita said.

Heaven snorted and covered her mouth. Jada pointed at Nita. "You stop being funny. Now I have to redo her lipstick, and quit pulling at that collar before you break the buttons."

Nita rolled her eyes. Lace and ruffles swished as she changed positions. Jada shook her head.

"You've got a handful in that one. Too much attitude, and she's not even a teenager yet."

Heaven glanced at Nita. She looked like an angel in her tulle ball gown with cap sleeves, her dark hair swept up from her neck with a few tendrils hanging in the back and a lilac flower and baby's breath at the side of her head. True, the attitude could use checking. "Leave Nita alone. We're getting along better now, aren't we, Nita?"

Her soon to be stepdaughter shrugged.

"What did you mean Daddy is a blinking robot?" Heaven tried not to laugh again, but she had to hand it to Nita. The girl had broken some of the nervousness that had clung to Heaven ever since she woke up that morning. The day had finally arrived, and she was soon to be married.

Nita pushed her face toward Heaven, raised her hands, fingers straight and thumbs tight at the sides. She blinked rapidly. "Daddy is like this. Uncle Stefan said he's nervous, and every time Uncle Creed asks Daddy a question, Daddy blinks some more."

Heaven and Jada broke up. They couldn't help it. Heaven raised her hand to cover her mouth again, but Jada caught her. She looked at her palm and saw that she had smudged her lipstick the first time. After a few minutes, Heaven got herself together. She touched a finger to the corner of each eye and sighed.

"I needed that." She fanned her face. "I just hope he loosens up by the time we take pictures and video. You'd think this would be old news to him since it's the second time."

Her friend hugged her. "Why shouldn't he be nervous? He's marrying the woman he loves, my beautiful friend, who deserves this happiness."

Heaven hadn't shared with her friend that theirs was basically a marriage of convenience, to give the kids a stable home. She'd let Jada believe an old love had been reignited, and since they both found themselves in the right place in their lives, Damen had asked her to marry him and she had said yes.

The door opened, and Shada came in. Heaven had feared Shada's anger toward her after she had run to tell Creed about the baby. Shada had just waggled at finger at her a few days later and said, "I'm going to have to watch you. You're a sneaky one."

The comment had been light, and Heaven figured out that the first weight had been lifted off Shada's shoulders. She was beginning to accept that she would have a loving family with all the insecurities that came with it.

"Oh, you look so beautiful, sis. Damen is going to have a fit."

Heaven started in surprise. She had never had a sister or a brother. "S-sis?"

"I'm testing it out," Shada said. "We're going to be sisters-in-law."

Heaven's eyes widened as Shada held up the ring. "You took it back?"

"I didn't have a choice. I was starting to suspect Creed might kidnap me and threaten not to let me free until I went through with it. He said in no uncertain terms am I going to be a single woman when our baby is born. So damn controlling, he makes me mad."

Jada sniffed. "I want to be a Marquette. All y'all are so cute!"

Heaven shook her head. "Did you forget you're married, and you love your husband?"

Jada rolled her eyes. "I can dump him."

"I'm going to tell Marco you said that."

Jada waved a hand. "Go ahead. The man knows better than that. Besides, we're too old to start over."

"How old are you?" Nita wanted to know.

"Be quiet, you," Heaven told her. "You don't ask older ladies their age."

"Why not?"

"Because we're liable to get blinky to hold back the tears." Jada imitated Damen, and they were all cracking up again.

"What's so funny?" Shada demanded. "I want to know too so I can laugh."

Heaven looked at Jada, and Jada looked at Nita. "Ask your niece."

"What?" Shada insisted.

Heaven explained, and Shada almost shouted in laughter. "Y'all better leave Damen alone. He can't help himself. Wait, never mind. I'm going out there to make fun of him."

Heaven grabbed her arm to stop her. "Don't do that."

Shada winked. "Me and Damen have had our issues. If I don't embarrass him, he'll think I'm going soft. I have to do it, Heaven. Don't hold me back."

"For me," Heaven begged. "You can dig at him when we get back from our honeymoon."

Shada groaned. "Fine, but I'm going to tell the videographer to get some extra close-up shots of the groom." She slid out the door before Heaven could stop her.

"That's a hardcore one," Jada commented. "She's going to make a great sister. I'm so happy for you, Heaven. You deserve this and more."

Tears pricked Heaven's eyes, but she swallowed the emotion. "Thank you, Jada. Well, I guess we're ready to go. Let's do this."

Heaven stood in front of Damen in the most beautiful white dress she had ever laid eyes on. The lace ball gown with beaded appliqué around the neckline and a deep V back fit her curves just right, although they had to call in a seamstress at the last minute to make adjustments. Shada had claimed the food she prepared over the days of preparation for the wedding was so good Heaven couldn't help gaining weight.

Heaven knew the food remark was true, but what made even more sense was that she felt safe. Marquette's was jam-packed with well-wishers and family and friends. Security guarded the corners of the place, gazes sharp. Heaven had noticed all of this in passing. What she focused on now as she stood before the altar was her fiancé.

The nervousness had faded from Damen's visage and actions. All she saw was the man who had been there for her, who protected her and fathered her son with her. He was sexy and strong in his dark tux, and his green eyes shined bright with joy behind his glasses. Her heart stuttered in her chest, and when Damen held out his hand, she placed hers into his palm.

"I, Damen Marquette," he said, "give to you, Heaven Burk, this ring, as a symbol of my commitment to love…"

He paused at the word love, and Heaven swallowed, staring at their joined hands. Damen gave hers a gentle squeeze and a tug. She looked up at him to find him staring back, and he repeated his vows. "To *love*, honor, and respect you."

Someone in the audience sobbed, and Heaven suspected it was Jada. Tears rolled down her own cheeks, and she sniffed. She wasn't imagining it. Damen emphasized the word love, and as she listened to him, her heart swelled.

"I choose you, Heaven, above all others, to be my wife."

Above all others. The words resounded in her mind again and again, threatening to make her explode in sheer joy. She had thought this day would be just a ceremony as the words of their vows said, a symbol, but it was more than that. Each word she and Damen spoke held meaning, and now as they finished speaking their promises to one another, the minister announced, "You may kiss the bride."

Damen guided her into his arms and kissed her deeply. Heaven melted against his chest, letting him trap her hands between them. His fingers slid along her sides to her hips and threatened to continue around to her butt, but she caught him and drew him away. A cheer with laughter rose from the audience.

"I present to you Mr. and Mrs. Damen Marquette."

Gideon ran forward and threw his arms around Heaven. She hugged her son and bent down to kiss his cheek. "Mom," he whispered, "you look really great."

"Thanks, baby." She kissed him again.

Nita wandered over to Damen, and he drew her into a hug and a kiss that she squirmed away from. Gideon stuck his hand out to Damen, who brushed it aside and swept his son into his arms. Gideon looked like he was on cloud nine. Her son would probably never get enough of Damen's attention. Damen had suggested they take the kids with them on a brief weekend honeymoon. Then at winter break, they would do a longer family getaway to Cancun. She had agreed since they were all so new. The more time together, the better.

Since the reception was taking place on the second floor, there was no need to go anywhere. Heaven accepted all the well wishes and hugs and then turned toward her husband to find him watching her. She smiled and raised her eyebrows. "What?"

"You're—"

A commotion rose in the back near the restaurant's entrance. Damen broke off and frowned in that direction. When the two of them spotted the bodyguards on the move, Damen drew her closer to his side.

"What's going on?" She stretched to her toes to see, but several of the guests were taller than her and stood in the way.

A man came into view, tall and scraggly with a full beard and long greasy hair. Pete reached for him, but the man dodged and started along the aisle. Several of the guests cried out in alarm and darted out of the way. Damen shoved Heaven behind him along with Nita.

"Gideon, get behind me," Damen ordered, but Gideon took on a fighting stance as if he would help fend off the madman.

Heaven reached out and dragged her son to her side with one hand and Nita to the other side. Nita clutched at her, eyes wide. Heaven figured the girl must be scared if she was willing to hold onto Heaven. Why was this happening on her wedding day?

"Guy, get him, damn it!" Damen barked.

Heaven looked out from behind Damen's wide back just as the giant bodyguard slammed the intruder face first on the floor. Weaver joined him on the other side, holding the man's arm in a punishing grip behind him. The entire room quieted down as Heaven guessed everyone wanted to hear what was being said.

The man groaned in pain. "Is this how you treat family?"

Creed burst through the crowd from somewhere and thrust Pete aside, who hovered above the other two guards. "Let him up!"

"Who is that dirty man, Daddy?" Nita inquired in the lull.

For some reason, Gideon scowled at her. She stuck her tongue out at him, and Heaven felt Damen starting to relax as the guards pulled the man to his feet. Creed and Damen stared at the man, but Stefan darted forward and drew him into a hug, slapping his back. "It's been too long."

The man shrugged and flashed a white smile amid the excess of hair. "Yeah, it has, Stefan. You haven't changed. Creed and Damen, you guys scared of me, or what? Your fancy bodyguards almost dislocated my shoulder."

Creed took his time stepping forward, and he folded his arms over his chest, annoyance simmering. "I didn't expect you to show up here after I bailed you out—for the hundred time, I might add."

"What's a buck or two amid family?" The man spread long arms out to the side, unrepentant of the inconveniences he'd apparently caused Creed.

Damen moved closer. "You've been helping him, Creed? You never said."

"Didn't you know?" The man slapped Creed on the shoulder. "Creed's the unofficial head of the family, and I am family. So where's the beautiful bride? That's why I'm here after all, to meet my new cousin."

Heaven gasped. "Cousin?"

Damen turned and drew her to him. He seemed less than enthusiastic about introducing her, but he did anyway. "This is my wife Heaven and our son Gideon. Heaven, Gideon, this is my cousin Duke Marquette, the thorn in the our family's side."

"Heaven," Duke barked excitedly. He started forward as if he would hug her. "Welcome to the family."

Damen stepped in front of him, blocking his path. "Touch her, and I'll do what Guy didn't."

Duke chuckled. "Whoa, our little Damen has grown up. I thought you were against violence."

"You'd be surprised what I would do for Heaven."

"Spoken like a man in love."

Heaven cleared her throat, embarrassed. "It's nice to meet you, Duke."

"Likewise. Looks like my cousin did good the second time around. Never liked that—"

"Duke," Creed ground out. "You're late, and you've got a big mouth."

Nita was staring curiously up at Duke, and he had just been about to insult her mother. Heaven didn't know what to make of the man. He looked like he'd just spent the last month sleeping in an alley, but at least he didn't smell like it. She studied his face. He needed a shave, a haircut, and a shower, but no mistake about it. Duke had the Marquette green eyes and the arrogant nose and jaw line. He was family. Where had they been keeping him?

Jada came along and grabbed Heaven's hand. "Come on. Let's get you out of this dress and into something more comfortable."

Damen touched her belly with one hand and looked into her eyes. "I wanted to have a quick chat with my wife."

Warmth rushed through Heaven, and she smiled before offering him a feathery kiss on the lips. "Wait for me. I'll be right back."

She slipped away, and her head was full of thoughts of Damen the whole time she changed. Jada chattered nonstop, but Heaven couldn't help replaying Damen's vows in her head and how he had said he would do anything for her. Was it just about Gideon, or was she reading more into it? She knew what her heart believed, but the stupid thing wanted to take leaps and bounds beyond reason.

Jada tapped Heaven's shoulder. "Are you listening to me? Never mind. Don't answer that. All you can think about is getting back to your husband."

Heaven drew in a shaky breath. "My husband. Is that weird or what, Jada?"

"It's not weird. It's great, and you'll get used to it soon enough and start calling him fool."

Heaven laughed. "I will not."

Her friend cackled. "I'm just kidding, but I know how you feel. This is new and wonderful and scary at the same time. All I know is he looks like the sensitive type."

"Sensitive?" Heaven thought about it. "I guess you're right. Damen was always pretty blunt about blurting out his thoughts, but he was never unkind and always thinks of others. He's so sweet."

"You love him?"

"Yeah, I love him very much."

"I know you, Heaven." She pointed a finger at Heaven. "You're scared he doesn't love you, but he married you."

She nodded, too unsettled to say why.

"It's not about the kids."

Was the freaking woman reading her mind?

"It's about a man and a woman. He is the sensitive type, and nobody needs that kind like you need it. You tried to hide how bad it was with that asshole Leon, but we could guess. We didn't know how far he crossed the line, but we knew he wasn't the nicest to you in private. I tried to get you to leave and offered you a place to stay."

"I know." Heaven heaved a sigh. "I just didn't want to drag anyone else into my problems."

"Now you've got Damen. He looks like the real deal, Heaven. Hold onto him, and if there's ever any misunderstandings, talk it out together. I want to see you completely happy and satisfied. Else, I'm flying back down and busting his balls for him."

"Ouch." Heaven laughed. "You saw what happened with their cousin. Really think you have a chance with the bodyguards?"

"I don't know. I feel like I want to try something anyway. They're so big and muscular. Yummy."

"Remember Marco?"

Jada growled. "I should have stayed single. Crap, what am I saying? You're all set. Go find your husband and let him convince you he loves you."

Heaven let Jada shuffle her out the door. She hadn't meant to give the impression she was unsure of Damen's love, but it must have been written all over her face. He had admitted he loved his ex, might still love her, but he had also offered himself to Heaven to have for always. Maybe Heaven should tell him what she really wanted.

"Psst, Heaven."

She stopped and looked behind her. Damen stood at the office door signaling to her. Heaven headed back his way and tumbled forward as her husband hurried her into the office. He encircled her in his arms and backed her to the door, trapping her with his body. Heaven brought her hands up to his face and stroked along his jaw. Her heart beat faster, and she leaned in to nibble his bottom lip. He smelled so good, and already she felt his hard-on pressed against her belly.

"We're not having sex in here," she announced.

He grinned. "I wasn't planning on it. Not that I'm not tempted, but I've heard stories about Creed and Shada."

"Ew." She managed to get out of his hold and walked over to his area. "They didn't do it on your desk, did they?"

"Probably not."

She glared at him. He smirked.

"Why do I have the feeling you're just pretending to be

grossed out by the thought?"

"I never said I was grossed out." He strode over to lean against the desk and patted his chest. "I need you in my arms."

She tried to keep the smile hidden from her face but melted into his hold. Damen's fingers danced along her spine, sending chills of delight racing over her skin. She nuzzled his chin and kissed it then sought his lips. He slanted his mouth above hers and parted her lips. Heaven welcomed his tongue into the warm recesses of her mouth, eager for more. Her pussy throbbed to be filled with his dick, but she knew that would come later when they were alone.

After some time, she drew back and flattened her palms on his chest. She tried to look into his eyes but failed because she was so damn nervous. "Damen."

"Hmm?"

"Um, you said…" Courage failed her, but she blew out a breath and dredged up more from her toes. She was glad he waited in silence rather than rush her. "You told me your body is mine, right?"

"Yes, and we solidified it today."

"What if I don't—"

"Don't want my body? I'm not convinced." He plucked a taut nipple she didn't even realize he'd seen. Heaven smacked his hand away.

"No, that's not what I mean, Mr. One-Track Mind."

He chuckled, and she realized he'd just used it as an excuse to do what he just did.

"What if I want more than your body?" *Oh jeez, I shouldn't even be asking him this five minutes after we're married. We had an agreement. I can't ask for more.*

"Tell me what you want, Heaven."

She dared to peek up at him. His beautiful eyes were trained on her, calm, self-assured. She waited a beat, and he pushed his glasses higher with two fingers. Her heart fluttered.

"What if I told you I want your heart too?" She raised her chin higher. "What if I said I want you to love me, to be *in* love with me and *only* me?"

"Hm, that's an interesting concept."

"It's not a concept!" His continued amusement pissed her off, but she had come this far, and she couldn't turn back. Damn it to hell, she loved him. She loved him over a decade ago, and that love might have died down or disappeared over the years. Their reconnect and the way he treated her these days brought it all back with a vengeance. Heaven began to think Damen had influenced some of the changes in her. She could have gotten the ball rolling by moving to New Orleans, he gave the decision momentum. Either way, she was bolder, stronger, and determined to speak up for herself. She wanted what she wanted, and she needed to make it crystal clear. "I want your heart, Damen!"

"Oh, my sweet Heaven." He leaned closer to her face and kissed her cheek as one would a child. "That's impossible."

She stiffened.

"I can't give you what I don't have." He drew back and looked into her eyes. She tried to move, but he held her trapped against him. Their bodies met from her belly down. Her airway was beginning to close. If she passed out, would he let her hit the floor for being stupid enough to push for more than they agreed on? No, Damen wasn't like that. He'd catch her every time, even if he was pissed off at her, and that's what made it so hard to be with him like this.

A coldness washed over her. "Oh. I should have

known…"

Damen brushed a thumb across her lower lip. She swallowed.

"Heaven, when I first met you, you were like a breath of fresh air. I was awkward and gangly and too full of my own intelligence. You swept it all away in an instant because when I spoke to you, I forgot who I was. You were from another world, or a star, and I craved you so badly."

She pulled her mouth away from his touch. "I already know how much you want me physically."

"No. You don't."

Heaven glared through a sheen of tears.

"You can't understand, but I don't mind showing you each day. Besides, it's more than that. As I said, you were something different to me, an enigma I had to figure out. I didn't understand what I was feeling. You could almost call it an obsession. I identified it back then as lust. You disappeared before I could figure you out for myself."

She didn't speak again but lowered her gaze. The lump hadn't lessened in her throat but lodged there like it had become a permanent fixture. Well, this wasn't the first time she had been hurt. Maybe over time she could learn to stay with him and let it be enough. She wouldn't back out or give him up. That part was firm in her mind.

"Heaven?"

"What?" She snapped the word, irritated and hurt at the same time.

Damen touched his forehead to hers. "It looks like you still don't understand." He drew in a breath and blew it out. "Let me make it plain. I can't give you my heart when you already have it. I don't own my heart. You do."

Heaven's mouth fell open. Grinning like a damn idiot,

Damen shut it with one finger. The bastard. He had to know he'd scared the hell out of her and tore her apart. She put space between their faces and frowned into his. That's when she saw it. Damen let the mask fall away. Damen—her husband—hid his emotions behind jokes and good humor.

He loved her. Heaven remembered the time she had caught the look in Creed's eyes when he looked at Shada. She recalled the jealousy that had washed over her to think of a man feeling for her the way Creed felt about Shada. Here was Damen, expression wide open, showing her he cared.

Just in case, she said, "Say it. I want to hear the words."

He cupped her face with both hands. "I love you, Heaven. I loved you then, but I didn't know what it meant to love a woman like I love you. I loved you when I met my ex and when I came to love her, I still loved you."

She wrinkled her brow. "Are you serious? How can you be sure?"

"Because you've always been there. I felt guilty, like I was betraying her. I didn't let myself fantasize about you, but I was fully aware I held you in a special secret place. No one but me knew I hadn't gotten rid of you completely."

"Damen, I don't know what to think about that. I feel bad for her."

"Don't." He frowned in confusion. "Or do if you want. Don't misunderstand me. I convinced myself you were gone for good because that's what you wanted. I believed the life I lived after that was the life I would continue to lead, and Vida would be a permanent part of it. That's why I was able to love her and why I was able to be...affected...so harshly when she left."

Affected, he said. She smiled because Damen was still a man who didn't feel comfortable sharing all his feelings. He'd been hurt by his ex-wife leaving him. Now she understood it a little better herself. Damen loved her, and she left. He thought his life with Vida would be different. Instead, Vida left too. That's why Damen had pushed for her and him to get married practically the moment they met again.

"You refused to let me get away again," she said.

He made a noise of agreement.

"I admire you, Damen."

He groaned. "I'd rather you say you love me."

She laughed. "I love you."

He snatched her close and kissed her lips for a long, dizzying time. After a few frenzied heartbeats, he released her to speak.

"I was going to say, before I was rudely interrupted," she teased, "that I admire you because in the face of me leaving and Vida, you didn't give up."

He shook his head. "Oh, no, baby. I did give up. I was what you call a player for a long time. Women were for physical pleasure, and even if I didn't sleep with them, I flirted. It's what I did. Then I made a friend who blatantly told me I had my head in the sand, nursing a broken heart, and I needed to deal with it. She said I was too old to not deal with my emotional issues and that I was clinging to the past."

Heaven laughed. "Wow, blunt. Who was that?"

"Shada's sister."

"Really? You have to tell me about her."

"Not now," he insisted. "Right now, I'm thinking of a way to get you out of here so I can make love to you for the rest of the day."

"We have guests, sir."

"They will understand, especially my brothers."

"No way." She wiggled out of his arms and started toward

the door. "We have to cut the cake and thank everybody for sharing our day with us."

He groaned where he leaned on the desk. Heaven reached a hand out to him. As she did, her heart swelled, ready to burst out of her chest. *He loves me, he loves me,* she chanted in her head like a child.

"Coming, husband?"

"Mmm, I like the sound of that. "Yes, wife, I'm coming. Wait, how soon can that be literally true?"

She rolled her eyes, and they returned arm in arm to their guests.

CHAPTER THIRTEEN

"I didn't expect this," Heaven said as she hit a few keys on Damen's piano. They had the whole house to themselves because Shada and Creed had the kids. "I can't believe Creed agreed."

Damen handed her a drink, and she took a sip before he claimed her lips in a kiss. "It's just for one night. Shada wants to see what it's like and see if as she says she won't 'lose her damn mind.'"

Heaven laughed. "That sounds like her."

"Why are we in here?" He frowned at the room she liked, with hardwood floors, arm chairs, a fireplace, and even a couple bookshelves built into the wall with more knickknacks than books filling them.

"I like this room, but why do you have a piano?"

He shrugged. "I thought I'd learn to play. Turns out I love the guitar too much."

"You're ridiculous."

He grinned. "Well, then Gideon might want to someday. It will be here if he does."

Heaven sighed. "Sometimes I worry about him."

"Don't." He tugged her to her feet and led her into the hall. "If I'm right, Gideon's genius lies in a different direction than book smarts."

She frowned. "What do you mean?"

"I think music speaks to him on a level most of us could never understand."

"Like a prodigy?"

"If he played, probably yes. He learned what I taught him in an instant, but I suspect he's not going in that direction."

"How so? You've lost me."

Damen paused by a settee in the hall, and she wondered why the hall even needed one. Who cared? She loved this historical styled house and wouldn't change a thing other than Gideon's room. "Composition, production, Gideon might enjoy it all, and I want to see how far he can go. Not like my dad did, working in dives for pennies and drinking it away. We have the means to help our son, Heaven, and I want to do it. Are you with me?"

"Definitely."

"Good. Now about this sexy body right here…" He slid a hand over her belly, and she caught his wrist.

"We can't do it in the hall."

"It's our house. Why not? No one's around." He wiggled his eyebrows. She shook her head at him. Heaven turned to run off, but Damen caught her and drew her backward into his arms. The man had the buttons undone on her pants in a heartbeat and his hand inside her panties. "What do we have here?"

"My cootchie. Get out of there."

"Never." She gasped when he parted her folds and slid a finger inside her. Damen groaned. "You're already wet."

"I'm n-not," she lied and sagged against him. He stroked into her heat and out again, driving her desire higher. At the same time, he squeezed her left breast through her blouse and bra and then, unsatisfied, he shoved the material aside to pinch her nipple. She whimpered. "Damen, the bodyguards."

"They've been ordered to give us space."

"They won't go far." She moaned again when he began circling her clit.

Damen loosened her pants even more and pushed them along with her panties over her hips. Anybody arriving would get an eyeful, but her husband didn't care. He kept rolling a thumb over her bud until she was shaking with a need to release. Her pussy throbbed, and her inner muscles coiled in anticipation of it.

"Open your legs a little more, Heaven."

"Damen."

"A little more, baby."

She complied, and he pushed four fingers into her heat. He worked them in and out while holding her to his chest, one breast engulfed by his palm. The man refused to stop but increased his pumping into her slick sex until she forgot about the bodyguards.

"Damen, I'm going to come!"

He groaned in her ear. "You're so wet, that's exactly what I'm waiting for."

"We could have...we..." She lost her train of thought. An orgasm shattered all resistance, and she screamed in pleasure. From the hall, which was a wide-open space, her voice echoed all over the house. She had expected Damen to cover her mouth, but the bum let her go for it.

Before Heaven could come down from her high, she heard steps on the second floor. Damen moved behind her, but instead of ending their lovemaking session, he whisked her around to face the wall and the settee. She had a moment to gather a breath and then he plunged his cock into her pussy from behind. Heaven cried out his name. He held onto her hips and pushed deep. She tumbled forward, one knee on the settee, a hand on the wall. Damen followed and didn't allow their bodies to part for a second.

"They'll see," she whispered, but her eyelids were heavy from the pleasure of him being inside her.

Damen encircled her in his arms. He curved his body over hers, molding to her butt and shoving her blouse and bra up to cup her breasts. "They wouldn't disrespect us that way."

"We're in public."

"We're in the privacy of our home, and I'm going to make love to my perfect wife all over this house."

"Damen," she protested one last time.

He covered her mouth with his and pushed his tongue between her lips. She couldn't help sucking lightly on his tongue. Damen allowed it for a few seconds and then drew back. "Tell me you love me, baby. I want to hear it again."

He pumped into her, their skin sticking from perspiration. Heaven loved the hardness of his thighs and the heat from his body. She let the fear go. "I love you, Damen."

"I love you too, Heaven." He moved his hand from her breast to her belly and lower to cover her mound as his dick glided in to the hilt. "Can I come in you?"

She looked back at him, eyes wide. He stilled, waiting. She swallowed and nodded, and then Damen was pumping deep into her pussy. His breath came in short, noisy bursts as he pushed, and bent forward, arching her back, and taking all of him. Damen jerked, and his hot seed flooded her sex.

"Damn, that felt good," Damen moaned. He pulled her up and slid out of her. They both moaned and kissed. Her husband turned her to face him. "I don't think I've had enough."

"Upstairs this time," she demanded.

He sighed. "Fine. You win."

They started hand in hand toward the stairs. Heaven scarcely got her pants pulled up enough to walk straight let alone avoid flashing anyone. A familiar ding sounded throughout the house, and they both froze.

"Crap, who's that?" she squeaked.

"I'll see."

Heaven held onto him. "Your junk is hanging out, and so is mine, and we're…gooey."

He chuckled. Damen spun around to face her and whipped her into his arms. He took the stairs at a jog and reached the top in seconds. "Guy, the door," he called out.

"Yes, sir."

Heaven looked around to see where the bodyguard spoke from, but Damen whisked her into their bedroom, kicked the door shut, and laid her on the bed. She had enough time to slide to the edge of the bed when there was another knock on the bedroom door. Heaven frowned. "Wasn't this supposed to be our alone time?"

Damen seemed just as confused about the interruption. He stood looking down at the front of his pants as if he tried to determine whether to take them off or zip them up. "Who is it?"

"I'm sorry to disturb you, Mr. Damen," Guy called through the door. "But there's a man here who claims to be

Ms. Heaven's father."

Heaven blinked in disbelief. "That's not possible."

"Professor Alfred Burk," Guy said.

Heaven glanced at her husband, who hadn't spoken since Guy announced who was at the door. She studied his expression and knew right away, he wasn't surprised by the announcement. She stood up and faced him, hands on her hips. "You knew he was coming, didn't you?"

Damen tried touching her cheek, but she ducked her head away. "I didn't know. I hoped he would days ago."

"What?"

He sighed. "Remember when you asked me what I was up to? This is what. I contacted him and had a long discussion with him about you. I tried to invite him to come down and give you away, to behave for once like a father should. Don't be mad, Heaven, baby."

Her mouth fell open. "I'm not mad. I can't believe you did that for me. He was your friend."

"You're my wife. There's nothing I want more than to make you happy."

She wrapped her arms around his waist. "I can't get over how amazing you are."

He raised her chin and frowned down at her. "If you want me to send him away, I will. I realize maybe I jumped the gun, and I shouldn't have pushed. He might have ruined our wedding day if he showed up without any warning. I can make sure he never hurts you again."

She laughed. "That sounds like you're the mob, and you'll get the boys to 'make him disappear.'"

"Hm, maybe I should develop mob connections next."

She smacked his arm, and he grinned.

"No, I don't hate him, Damen, as much as I kind of wish

I did. He showed up, so I'll see what he has to say for himself. If he's critical of me and tells me I'm not good enough for you, I'm having Weaver toss his ass out on the front lawn."

Damen kissed the top of her head. "That's my girl. Don't worry. One false word, and Guy will help Weaver do it. Fair enough?"

"Fair enough. But first, my dad can wait until I take a shower. I'm not going down there smelling like sex."

Damen followed her toward the bathroom. "Well, you're looking a little tense. Let me help you."

"I don't believe you."

He held up one hand and laid the other over his chest. "Honestly, the best way to relieve stress and tension is through lovemaking in the shower. Come on. Let me show you."

"Damen Marquette, you're impossible."

"Yes, I am."

The End